LPM008

D1288036

THE EDEN MYSTERY

Interstellar entrepreneurs, the Eden clan, had opened up new planets, building a galactic empire, governed by the United Worlds' Federation. However, stability is threatened by an impending war between the worlds of Technos and Mogul. The Federation fears intervention by the clan's sole survivor, Kyle Eden. Meanwhile, Hew Keston is investigating the Eden family's history for the media corporation Stereoscopic Inc. But his life is in danger — someone is stopping him from learning the secrets of the Eden clan!

SYDNEY J. BOUNDS

THE EDEN MYSTERY

Complete and Unabridged

LINFORD
Leicester

First published in Great Britain

First Linford Edition
published 2009

British Library CIP Data

Bounds, Sydney J.
   The Eden mystery. - -
   (Linford mystery library)
   1. Space colonies- -Fiction.
   2. Suspense fiction.
   3. Large type books.
   I. Title II. Series
   823.9′14–dc22

   ISBN 978–1–84782–908–5

Published by
F. A. Thorpe (Publishing)
Anstey, Leicestershire

Set by Words & Graphics Ltd.
Anstey, Leicestershire
Printed and bound in Great Britain by
T. J. International Ltd., Padstow, Cornwall

This book is printed on acid-free paper

1

Opportunity is a fine thing

Hew Keston sat in a low uncomfortable tubular chair, his neck aching as his head swivelled from side to side, in an effort to focus his eyes and attention on Barnabas. Merlin X. Barnabas, programme chief for Stereoscopic Inc., paced the long indigo-ceilinged office from his mammoth desk to the wall screen and back again.

Watching him, a faint memory stirred in Keston, the memory of some research he'd once done on an archaic ball game — tenball? — where the spectators swivelled their heads left-right, left-right to follow a small white ball as it crossed and re-crossed a net.

He stretched out cramped legs in front of him as Barnabas paced restlessly, one large hand brandishing a fat green holder containing a burning cigar, talking fast at the top of his voice. Barnabas was always enthusiastic at the start of a new project, Keston thought sourly, but it wouldn't last. Enthusiasm would die long before the job was completed; yet still he was caught up by that ringing voice and held fascinated.

'This is your chance,' Barnabas boomed. 'This can put you in the big time.'

Keston felt the knot of sourness swell inside him. Once, he too had thought in terms of 'the big time', but not any more. He wasn't young enough to believe that crap now.

'The Eden Clan,' Barnabas said. 'I want you to do a full-length exposé with all the trimmings.'

Keston's ears pricked up, and his words came out sharper than he intended. 'Exposé? It was biography just now.'

Barnabas scattered ash as he flourished his cigar. 'Exposé, biography . . . just words.' He stopped pacing to pick out one disc from the library on his desk.

'Mercer's version, Eastlake's, pop-mythical, standard — there's a hundred of them and all different. I want the true Eden story. What really happened. And that's what you're going to give me.' He inserted the disc into a projector and started it operating.

Keston shifted his chair back to get a better view of the screen, He hadn't seen this recording before. Eden — which Eden? he wondered — headed a parade along the wide throughway of some off-Terran city. The legendary handsome Eden, sitting straight and proud in an ornate saddle, riding his single-horned Beast. He was surrounded by, almost submerged under, a flag-waving, streamer-throwing crowd, backed by exotic-looking architecture.

Barnabas had cut out the sound track and spoke above the silent stereoscopic image. 'It's big, the biggest story ever. How did they do it? One family, starting from nothing, totally unknown ... manipulating entire worlds ... taking a percentage here, a rake-off there ... gaining wealth, power, status ... and finally, their own planet. *This* is Clan Eden!'

Keston, watching the changing images on the screen, suddenly found his view blocked by the massive bulk of Barnabas. A finger stabbed at him. The booming voice lowered a notch.

'Status, did I say? Perhaps, and perhaps not. There's no shortage of people who hate the Edens, on a score of worlds, people who call them criminal, ruthless killers. All right, allow that for the argument — they're still the biggest criminals of all time! Imagine, whole worlds out there . . . ' Barnabas gestured to the high window and the stratojets streaming past. 'It's the biggest, and I want it for Stereoscopic — what really happened — what the Edens are really like.'

Brooding, Keston said: 'That might not be so easy. The legend's got a strong hold now. There's so much material, so many different versions, who's to say which is imagining and which true? The old records, if they still exist — '

Barnabas crushed out his cigar, waved a hand magnanimously. 'Expenses, you'll be getting expenses. Visit every world the Edens went to, interview everyone who knows anything at all, backtrack them, dig out the dirt. Find the records, study the court trials. Search. Sift.'

Keston's lips moved silently, derisively. Barnabas could talk glibly about expenses now — it would be different when he sent them in.

'Maybe it won't be as hard as you think.' Barnabas switched off the recording and resumed his pacing. 'Kyle Eden, the last of the clan, what does *he* do? Squats on that sunless wanderer of his, never budging from one year's end to the next, a recluse. With this trouble between Technos and Mogul threatening to blow the Federation apart, with a hundred-odd worlds waiting for him to act, he does nothing. Why? Maybe because the Edens are finished.'

Keston felt his body go rigid with shock. The legend had been accepted dogma for so long that the idea of it ever ending seemed almost blasphemous. Yet it was true that Kyle Eden never left his own planet, and had not done so since he was a young man.

Barnabas snatched a memo from his desk as he passed. 'Here's your itinerary.

You'll go to Park first — that's where the first Eden's break came. Remember the laser handgun?' Keston nodded. 'See what you can dig up. Track him from there. Perhaps I can fix you a personal interview with Kyle later — it's not impossible.'

Barnabas was right, Keston thought, if he could pull this off . . . He wasn't unknown; he had a long string of second features to his name. But this was big, this was opportunity with a capital 'O'. If he got this story, he'd be right at the top as a scripter.

Barnabas said, abruptly business-like: 'Seventy thousand and expenses, agreed?'

'All expenses?'

'All those certified by our accountant.'

Keston hesitated only fractionally. Stereoscopic's accountant would be tight, he didn't doubt . . . but curiosity gripped him now. He wanted to know what the Edens were really like. 'Agreed!'

Barnabas thrust out a big hand, smiling. 'Good stetting!'

It was dismissal. Keston rose from his chair and gripped the hand, then turned and walked out of the office, along a passage to the lifts. He waved a casual greeting to a couple of staff scripters. The cage dropped swiftly to an underground roadway and he boarded a moving belt. Neon ad-signs flashed at him as he was carried under the city:

BUY SUPERSAVES! GET HEPTONE! TAKE FIXERS

He leaned into the wind with a hundred other commuters as the roadway rolled silently through the long tunnel. It was a smooth ride; Terrans had long since adjusted to riding the moving strip. His mind was flushed with Barnabas's enthusiasm. Eden. Where did he begin to dig into a story like that?

As he travelled, colour-ads blazed around him in continuous succession: WEAR READIMADES ... TODAY'S BEST IS RENTA-DREAM!

Keston felt the need for a drink and stopped off at an undercafe. He took a stool at the narrow counter running alongside the track and punched for a beaker of *Old Rye*; decided it was stupid to drink on an empty stomach and chose a real burger sandwich. It was expensive, but he was tired of everlasting soya steak. He ate hungrily, reciting the House of Eden genealogical chart in his head:

'In the beginning was Alain, who begat a son in his own image called Morg. And Alain died, and Morg begat a son likewise, called David. But Morg's days were numbered too, and David begat a son, Kyle . . . '

And Kyle was the last, Keston thought, the last of the line of a family of famous — or infamous, depending on your viewpoint — entrepreneurs spanning more than a century of active life. And that century the most flamboyant in galactic history.

The wall screen of the undercafe switched to —

'NEWS FLASH SPECIAL! United Worlds headquarters still refuse to make any comment on the current critical situation. With Mogul and Technos manoeuvring to extend their respective spheres of influence, in direct contravention of the non-intervention pact, the Federation is threatened with fission. On every planet throughout the galaxy, people are asking: when will Eden show his hand? What will he do? What *can* he do?'

A topical opening for his script? Keston wondered. Or would it serve better as an epilogue?

The screen changed as another flash came on: 'TONIGHT! Clan Eden supporters meet in Eden Hall at nineteen-thirty hours City time. Fifty credits gets you the very latest message from Kyle Eden in person — come one, come all!'

Keston smiled cynically, then thought: might as well drop in on them before he made the trip to Park, he might pick up a few ideas. He swallowed his drink, remembered to buy anti-stetting pills, and stepped back onto the moving roadway.

It carried him effortlessly past underground shopping arcades; BARGAIN MART — CREDIT COUNTER flashed the neons. Commuters joined and left at random; youngsters played the strip game, running headlong against the traffic. As he approached Eden Hall, clan supporters wearing *We're for Kyle* badges crowded the belt.

He stepped off with them and took the lift up, used his personal identity-credit seal to gain admittance. The hall was big and filling rapidly. Keston edged a way through the crowd, watching faces, listening.

Sound rose to the lofty ceiling and boomed back in waves from the walls. The fans were excited, keyed to fever pitch; a tension almost electric seemed to link them as they drifted, forming cliques, breaking up and forming others. This was the embodiment of the legend. Did they really believe it? Could they?

Keston manoeuvred round the hall; mainly teenagers, he noted the sexes equally represented, with very few of his own age group. Their dress was exotic. He passed a snatch of conversation: 'Of course Eden will — '

Will what? he wondered, moving on. He stealthily pulled a mini-recorder from his pocket and switched it on; maybe he could find a use for some of the current catch phrases. A larger-than-life size bust of Eden, ruggedly handsome in the best heroic tradition, overlooked the meeting from a dais; molded from a clear plastic, internal lighting gave it a spiritual quality. It dominated the hall.

An officious voice called for quiet and gradually the hum of conversation died. 'Here is a message from Kyle Eden — ' The outburst of cheering nearly deafened Keston: '*Clan Eden . . . Clan Eden . . . CLAN EDEN*!' He grimaced.

Silence followed slowly and, into it, faded the familiar voice of legend: 'To my followers on all worlds throughout the galaxy, greetings! Kyle Eden speaks to you in person . . . '

Keston snorted derisively, and a podgy man smelling of violets peered first at his face, then down at the mini-recorder.

'These are troubled times,' Kyle Eden said. 'Two opposing factions seek to split the Federation and destroy the status quo. Both selfishly strive to increase their power at the expense of others' freedom — worse, their own dissension could lead to war. Galactic war! They must not succeed. United Worlds must act!'

The recording finished amid a storm of

cheers and clapping. Phoney as hell, Keston decided, wondering who had scripted it. But the faces around him showed only animation and enthusiasm; except for the podgy man who had edged closer and stood watching him with an intent expression.

Irritated, Keston snapped. 'It's the script that smells, not me — take your deodorant someplace else!' He moved away.

Behind the dais, a curtain swished aside to reveal a wall screen. The officious voice returned: 'And now we shall continue the saga of Morg Eden from the point at which we left him last week.'

The screen glowed to life, showing one of the serf-cities of Anarchein, with a mob surging through the streets in a clash with armed police. At the crucial moment, Eden — a noble figure on his horned Beast — came riding into view, laser-gun in hand, to lead the oppressed in revolt against their tyrant.

His gun flashed brightly. As the beam speared into their ranks, the police agents melted away, to leave Eden surrounded by a cheering throng.

This was a real pop version, Keston thought in disgust. Naïve — it seemed incredible that anyone could believe stuff like this. Let them wait till they got *his* biography, the hard facts . . .

He pushed his way to the lift gates at the back of the hall, waited for them to open. Two teenagers, arriving late, brushed him aside with a casual, 'Outa the way, pop.'

Keston stepped into the empty cage, angry, glaring back. The fans vanished into the crowd but, through the closing gates, he saw the podgy man again — this time holding a tele-camera focused on *him*.

The lift plummeted down and Keston wondered uneasily about the podgy man: just who was he? Why was he so interested in him? What did he need a video record for?

There were no answers and, shrugging off his annoyance, Keston dismissed the man from his mind and stepped onto the west-bound roadway. Park tomorrow, he reminded himself.

He reached the apartment block and let himself into his service flat, a compact cubicle with wall stereo, a desk — considerably smaller than Barnabas's — a computer, and shelves of reference discs. A mirror reflected back his image as he prepared for sleep: swarthy skin with a beak of a nose, dreamy eyes and small stubborn lips. He brooded, scowling, on the paunch he was starting and promised, not for the first time, that he would take more exercise.

His glance fell, with some pride, on a row of his own recorded biographies: *Jamieson, exo-biochemist; Knightly, kinetic sculptor; Burke, a 27th Century missionary.* And now, the Edens . . .

Hew Keston pressed a button and the sleep cocoon unrolled from the wall and wrapped itself about him.

2

Trouble with seals

Light slanted in through the apartment window, hitting Keston's face and waking him. He rolled out of his cocoon and punched the button that restored it to its wall cache. Humming a number from the latest stereo musical, he showered and wiped away his overnight stubble with a depilatory cream.

Dressed in a casual outfit, he crossed to the window and looked out at the skyscraper canyons that made up the city; geometric blocks reached to the far horizon. He would be glad to leave Terra for a while, for a less depressing vista. He punched for breakfast, scowled as he saw it was the inevitable soya steak, and tipped it straight down the waste chute. He couldn't face that muck this morning.

Some men married and raised a family to give meaning to their life; Hew Keston had work that genuinely interested him and the driving ambition to make a name in his chosen profession. And today he was starting on the Eden story . . .

The quartz clock showed it was late, and he uncapped a small tube and swallowed an anti-stetting pill — stet travel always made him feel sick. He fitted a new tape in his mini-recorder, slipped it into his pocket and descended to the underground roadway. Neon-ads flashed past as he rode the strip; he was as unaware of them as he was of the other commuters riding with him. He made one change to reach his local stet station.

He stepped off the moving belt as a new sign showed: SPACE-TIME ENERGY TRANSMITTER — *Instant travel to any part of the galaxy.*

The station hall was vaulted and lined with rows of transmitting booths, busy with travellers coming and going. Keston joined a queue at the departure desk and waited his turn. Reaching the duty operator he said briskly, 'Park, please,' and impressed his personal seal to the logbook.

16

The uniformed operator checked the co-ordinates and power required against a routing chart, and pre-set the dials on a vacant booth.

Watching the operator's apparently casual movements, Keston felt apprehensive. He'd never got over his uneasiness of stetting, and reminded himself that his nervousness was completely irrational. But still he wondered: did an accident ever happen? Did some unfortunate traveller step into a booth — and simply disappear? No such accident had been made public to his knowledge . . .

'All set when you are,' the operator said in a bored voice.

Kenton's stomach muscles flinched as he took a step towards the empty booth; fortunately the anti-stetting pills would control his tendency to travel sickness. The door locked shut on him . . .

Stetting was vital to galactic civilization, Keston told himself. Ship travel, limited by the speed of light, was simply not good enough. Communications alone demanded instant travel.

The door opened — he had crossed the

17

barrier of the space-time continuum —
and he stepped out on another world,
halfway across the galaxy.

The arrival hall on Park bore a strong
similarity to the one he had just left, with
its rows of booths and reception desk; but
the light here was natural, flooding in
from high open windows. The air, too,
had a sharper fresher tang to it.

He signed in beneath a large mural
depicting a hunting scene — the old-
fashioned kind, with men stalking a lion
through jungle — inscribed: WELCOME
TO PARK.

'Here for the hunting, sir?'

Keston shook his head. 'Just doing
some research.' He walked through an
opening onto a high balcony for his first
view of Park, the hunters' paradise.

The reception hall, he discovered, was
housed in a tower. Blue-green grass
stretched in an undulating plain to the
distant horizon, dotted here and there
with trees and shrubs. A distant animal,
too small to identify, grazed among ferns.
Nearer, but out of sight, the barking of
hounds sounded. Although this was not

18

Terra, there was nothing alien about the view at first glimpse.

Keston leaned on the balcony rail, looking down. Immediately below him, tables were set out under a gay colored awning on a tessellated forecourt; here, out of the blinding sunlight, visiting hunters relaxed over drinks and indulged in small talk with one of the guides. Wealthy, powerful men from a score of worlds.

Studying them, reading the hunger in their faces, Keston shivered. He would not want to be a quarry. The mores were different on Park; this was a world where hunters went after the most cunning of all animals — man. His thought swerved onto an opposite track; what possessed any man to sign away his life? The fee was huge, of course, enough to set up the quarry's dependants in comfort for the next twenty years. But, even so, a man must be desperate . . .

And what was it that made the men sitting below so eager to hunt one of their own kind to his death?

Keston went down, bought himself a

drink at the bar, and carried it to an empty table. The guide looked at him, moustache twitching, sensing instinctively that he was no hunter.

Hunters' talk drifted across the terrace. 'Who's our quarry, guide? What do you know about him?'

'He's called Lomax — a hauler from Pedestar.'

Despite the heat of the outsize sun hanging in the sky, Keston felt chilled. Pedestar was one of the backward planets, where the less fortunate could only make an existence by selling their muscle — men used as beasts of burden to haul wagons. He imagined a hauler would not have much to live for anyway . . . but still the idea of the hunt disturbed him.

Since the discovery of stetting, by Van Heufel three centuries back, Earth-type worlds throughout the galaxy had been colonized in a mad rush by men of every different race, creed and party; twice a hundred diverse groups swarmed to the stars, each to perpetuate their own way of life. Fanatics of every kind fled Terra to set up a personal Utopia; vegetarians, advocates of free-love, neo-Christians, sun-worshippers, racial discriminators and those discriminated against — each community grabbed itself a planet on which to expand.

Each world insisted on self-government, that they were not mere colonies, and at first the only links between them were the traders. Quarrels flared up — and Terra finally proposed a loose Federation of the colonized planets with a non-intervention pact guaranteed by a United Worlds organization.

But some colonies progressed faster than others, faster than United Worlds anticipated — and now the balance was threatened by Technos and Mogul . . .

Keston took out his mini-recorder and switched it on. He spoke softly into it: 'Arrived on Park. First call on — '

He paused, thoughtful. It would need to be the Warden; a courtesy call. The Warden would suggest an informant, he hoped.

The guide, moustache twitching, left the hunters' table and walked across the

21

tiles to him, nursing an empty glass. 'You're no hunter,' he said flatly.

'Not your kind anyway. I'm hunting information for a script about the Edens.'

The guide drew up a chair and sat down. 'The Edens — Alain, you mean? That was way back. If it hadn't been for him, things would be very different here.' He gestured towards the horizon with his empty glass. 'Park was pretty wild in those days, overrun by predators — some of them big fellars. Fine country for real hunters, of course, but too dangerous to build up a tourist industry.'

Keston called for two more drinks, and the guide continued: 'Alain was a trader's rep, when traders were important people. He came to Park, selling a new model laser handgun, the ideal weapon for exterminating the big predators. And he was smart enough to turn down the offer of a good salary and stick out for a percentage of the profits . . . well, he cleaned up here, and left a rich man. That's how he got his start.'

Keston had left his recorder running. Now he said: 'Have any personal anecdotes been handed down about him?'

The guide grinned. 'One . . . it's always said he began life as tout for a Carnival joyhouse, you know. The story goes that when he arrived here, he brought one of the girls with him — a real eye-catcher — and used her to soften up his prospects. Then Eden would step in to clinch the deal. It could be true, I suppose.'

Distant, a gong reverberated, and the guide rose, smoothing his moustache. 'Lunch,' he announced. 'See you around, I guess.'

Keston followed the hunters through a wide doorway in the base of the tower. He'd had no breakfast, and the air of Park gave him an appetite.

He moved briskly along a passage. At the door to the dining room he collided with one of the waiters coming out in a hurry. For a moment, they merged in a wild tangle of arms and legs. Keston, off balance, staggered and clutched at the wall for support.

The waiter's face was averted, his voice muffled. 'Sorry sir, didn't see you coming.' Then he hurried away, and Keston caught only a glimpse of his back as he vanished round a corner.

Keston muttered a curse and went on into the dining room and took a seat on his own. The voices of the hunters, loud and arrogant, irritated him; but he soon found himself enjoying the meal. The meat was fresh and the flavour new to him — presumably the guides shot Park's wild animals for the kitchen.

He relaxed with a glass of the local brew, thinking about the story the guide had told him. Probably it wasn't true, but it suggested he might well visit Carnival next.

He watched a gangling man with a weathered face, wearing high boots and a bush jacket embroidered with a faded 'W', stalk catlike up to his table. 'Your personal seal, please.'

Keston reached into his pocket, in no way alarmed. The seals were artificially-created crystals, each one highly individual and impossible to duplicate; they formed the basis of the galactic identity-credit system. He handed over his without bothering to look at it.

The Warden's face tightened in bleak lines. 'I thought so — ' He waved up two burly guides hovering in the background. Hard muscular hands lifted Keston from his chair and held him firmly. The Warden said: 'You know perfectly well you shouldn't be in here — hunters and their quarry don't eat together.'

'Quarry?' Keston echoed, spine tingling with the first stirring of fear. 'I don't understand.'

The Warden rotated the seal between his fingers. 'This isn't yours, of course, Lomax? But then, they all say that — *after* they've signed!'

Keston stared at the seal, scalp rising. He moistened his lips. 'That isn't mine,' he protested. 'I can't imagine how it got in my pocket, unless — '

The Warden cut in, lips curling: 'All right, take him away — and work some of the fat off him.'

As the two guides dragged Keston, still protesting, from the dining room, a hunter's voice followed: 'That's the idea, Warden — must have our man at condition GO!'

Keston shouted back; 'I'm not Lomax, I tell you! It's all a mistake! I'm Hew Keston, a scripter for — '

'Shut it off,' one of the men holding him snapped. 'You've signed the release, now quit bawling!'

He was hustled along a corridor and pushed into a room, the door slammed and locked on him. Keston stared into the resigned faces of other quarries, and his nightmare grew. Blank hopelessness stared back at him. He swung round, badly frightened, and hammered at the door. 'I'm not a quarry,' he yelled. 'I'm not!'

He went on hammering until the door opened again and an angry guide pulled him out. 'For Eden's sake, you'll get 'em all worked up — c'mon, you for the exercise room. That'll quieten you down.'

Keston was pushed down the passage and into another room, strapped to a machine. 'I'm not Lomax,' he said, over and over, but the guide took no notice. He switched the exercise machine on, and left.

Keston's legs cycled and his arms

26

pistoned . . . round and round . . . in and out. The room was hardly more than a box, and steam-heated. He was left alone.

The heat seemed to increase and the air filled with steam. The machine went faster.

Sweat ran off him and he gasped for air. His legs and arms became one cruel ache, dulling his senses. After a time, he gave up shouting to conserve his flagging energy.

A blood-red haze hung before his eyes as he slipped into a semi-conscious state. The machine went on and on, relentlessly, exercising him. Time passed but he had no idea how much. Thirst nagged at his throat.

It must have been the waiter who had switched seals when they collided, he thought, but why? *Why?*

His torment went on till he felt hollow . . . legs cycling, round and round . . . arms pistoning, in and out. The heat was suffocating and the machine went faster, faster . . .

He began to think it would never stop

but, eventually, the exercise machine switched off and a guide released his straps. He tried to stand, and collapsed. He slept, and woke with a ravening hunger to eat the food placed before him.

The guide was the same one he had drunk with on the terrace, and seemed sympathetic. Keston said urgently: 'There really has been a mistake. Put through a call to Terra for me, to Stereoscopics Inc. Barnabas will confirm that he sent me here on a job — and you'll get something for your trouble.'

The guide stroked his moustache, hesitating — and as he hesitated, the Warden came briskly into the room. He prodded Keston critically. 'He'll do — give 'em a run for it now. Take him outside.'

Keston's protests went ignored. He was manhandled onto the forecourt below the tower, where the hunters waited with their guns; laser handguns, the same type that Alain Eden had imported into Park. The eyes of the hunters surveyed him, coldly, calculating. Keston shivered.

Two guides pushed him into a hover-cab and they set off, gliding between trees whose branches appeared to writhe; it was the first alien touch, and unnerving out of all proportion.

Keston turned to look at the guide driving the cab and saw, by his face, that a last appeal was useless. He glanced back, to the hunters following in a second cab.

They covered the plain swiftly and reached the edge of the rough, high grass and tangled vegetation climbing about giant trees, and stopped.

'Out,' ordered the head guide, and set his watch. 'You've got three hours start — get moving!' He gave Keston a push that sent him staggering into the rough.

Keston heard the howl of hounds straining at their leashes behind him. He began to run.

3

The Hunt

No one was going to help him, Keston realized; he had to find a hiding place and go to ground. After his first wild burst of speed, he slowed down, heart thumping. Olive-green foliage screened him from the hunters and he felt totally alone.

He crossed a patch of open grazing land in a blaze of hot sunshine and plunged into high grass; the needle-sharp blades slashed him, drawing blood, and he retreated hastily. He wondered: had any quarry ever eluded the hunters?

He jog-trotted through scrub, legs aching, a stitch in his side. Despite the exercise machine he was still not in good condition . . . and they believed he was a hauler! Water, he thought; follow a stream and use that to destroy his scent. He blundered through thickets, startling wild fowl that took off on flapping wings, cursing Barnabas and Eden and his own curiosity.

He found a trail left by some native animal and kept to it, hoping the animal's scent would confuse his own. He avoided a group of writhing trees; purple blossoms gave off an alien perfume that made him choke.

The sun rose higher and moisture steamed from broad leaves. His clothes stuck to him and he began to pant. The ground sloped away and he caught sight of a distant sparkle of water.

Behind him, a horn sounded and hounds began to bay; his skin tingled. The hunt was on! Keston felt his legs tremble as he forced another burst of speed, fighting down rising panic — only a clear head could save him now. He thrust between sticky clinging vines and came across another animal track — this time occupied.

The beast, small and armoured with sharp spines, lowered its triangular head and charged him. Keston hurled himself sideways, crashing full-length into the bushes, and lay still. The animal sniffed at him and passed by.

The baying of the hounds drove him on again, stumbling and sweating. Horns echoed, and a pulse drumbeat through his brain . . . *hunted* . . . *hunted*!

He went on till he came to running water. A momentary sense of relief claimed him, and he waded in, scooping up water in his cupped hands and drinking greedily. The water was cold, refreshing, in no way alien; his brain sharpened, he moved downstream beneath leafy overhanging boughs.

They might go the other way, he thought desperately; there was a chance at least.

The banks of the stream became stony and closely grown with thickets of spiky thornbush as he waded on. He picked a few berries, careless of consequences now, and chewed them, listening to the sounds of the hunt. They were closer, closing in on him, and he saw no point in struggling further. His only chance was to hide, and this looked as good a place as any.

He left the water and moved as carefully over the stones as if over eggs, trying to leave as little trail as possible, and forced a way into the thorn bushes. Sharp spikes stung his flesh; he burrowed in, crawling deeper, parting each stem carefully and ensuring that they sprang back in place after him. The hunters wouldn't find it easy to get at him; with luck, they might miss him completely.

Keston lay flat and waited, holding his breath. At the back of his mind, a vague idea formed — somehow he would sneak back and get to a stet booth . . .

The piercing blast of a horn, much nearer, brought him back to reality. He pressed his lips tightly together and breathed quietly. Fear crawled along his spine and stiffened the hairs on his neck. He heard the splash of moving boots in water. A hound sniffed at stones on the bank of the stream and howled. Sunlight rippled over the tangle of thorn stems and spikes, dappling them.

Not far off, a man cursed. A triumphant shout followed: 'The dogs have got his scent! He's gone to earth in the thornbrush — flush him out!'

Keston stifled a despairing sob and

scrabbled at the ground with his fingers; it was hard, too hard for him to make any impression, and he had no tool to dig with.

The vivid beam from a laser gun flashed, dazzling him, and the bushes caught fire. Flame crackled; smoke swirled in a thick dark fog.

'Now! Wait for him to run — watch for him!'

Keston sprawled flat, choking in smoke. The hounds barked excitedly. Another laser beam lanced into the brush nearby, and he hugged the ground. Angry red tongues of flame danced all around him; heat toasted him, and his lungs felt as if they would burst. He had to move or be burnt alive.

He staggered to his feet and lumbered into an unsteady run, burst through blazing thorn, swirling smoke hid him at first, then he was in the clear and running for his life.

The hunters were spread out in a wide circle and, as he plunged into a gap between two of them, one shouted: 'Lomax! There he goes — get him!'

A laser seared the ground behind Keston, scaring him to desperate effort. He ran, head down, arms pumping, faster than he'd ever moved before in his life. He gulped air in through his open mouth; his heart pounded like an overloaded machine.

Overhead, the whirring of rotor blades suddenly drowned out the hunters' cries. He jerked his head up to see a helicab swooping down and thought petulantly: it wasn't fair, using a helicab to hunt him from the air — it ought not to be allowed!

The helicab grounded just ahead of him. The blades stopped rotating and the cabin door opened; a man jumped to the ground, barring his way. Behind him, the hounds bayed frantically.

Keston slowed to a halt, exhausted. Escape was impossible now. He stood, with a sick feeling, waiting for the end, watching the man from the helicab stride authoritatively towards him. A thickset man, with cropped iron-grey hair, wearing a dun-coloured uniform.

He held out a small silver shield inscribed *United Worlds*, and asked, formally: 'Are you Hew Keston?'

Keston nodded dumbly, drawing air into his labouring lungs. It dawned on him that he had a chance to live; the UW organization was the closest thing to a galactic police force the worlds of the Federation knew.

He gasped out: 'Yes . . . *yes*! There's been a mistake — '

The United Worlds man nodded. 'So I've been told. Relax now, Mr. Keston. I'm Flowers, UW's local agent — leave me to handle this.'

The hunters came up, surly at the interruption. Guides held the hounds back on leashes. The head guide saw the UW markings on the helicab, and grunted: 'What is it?'

'This man is Keston, working for Stereoscopic,' Flowers said, 'not a quarry at all. You've slipped up somewhere — and I'm calling off this hunt while I investigate.'

A hunter, fingering his laser gun, grumbled: 'Some mistake — somebody's going to pay for this!'

The head guide slapped dust from his

bush-hat, disgusted. He faced the hunters. 'I'm sorry about this, gentlemen, but we can't go against a direct UW order. Park sincerely regrets the inconvenience — all your expenses will be taken care of. Now, I'll see about organizing transport back, and a fresh quarry.'

Flowers helped Keston into the helicab and took it up. As the ground fell away behind them and the figures of the hunters dwindled, Keston felt weak with relief. He could still hardly believe he was alive.

Belatedly, he turned to Flowers at the controls. 'Many thanks. If it hadn't been for you — '

Flowers shook his head. 'Not just me. You convinced one of the guides, and he contacted Barnabas, who got straight onto UW headquarters on Terra — they sent a messenger to me.'

Keston was impressed. People had moved fast to save him. Radio communication between the stars, restricted to light-speed, would have been useless. Only stet-messengers — personal carriers stetting between worlds — made instant communication possible. Without them, the Federation could not operate.

He felt a wave of gratitude. 'I'll see that guide gets a bonus,' he promised.

The helicab passed over the rough and set down on the forecourt of the reception centre. In front of the tower, the Warden, looking harassed, was waiting. Keston looked sourly at him.

'I don't understand at all how this deplorable mistake could have happened, Mr. Keston,' the Warden began, taking his arm. 'There has never been anything like it before. I shall look into the matter personally, you may be sure — meanwhile, your stay here, and anything you want, is on the house.'

Keston decided the first thing he wanted was a long cool drink. The next was off Park, fast. But he had to get his own seal back first . . .

Flowers dropped into a seat beside him. 'I'll be looking into it too — this seal-switch has all the earmarks of a deliberate murder attempt. D'you have any enemies you know of?'

Keston's scalp lifted. 'Murder? Enemies?

No . . . I don't know anyone who'd go that far.'

Flowers tried a new angle. 'You're here digging for data on Eden, is that right?' He pronounced the name distastefully, as if it were anathema. As a loyal UW man, Keston thought, Flowers would be hypersensitive about the Federation; for him, any intervention by Eden must be considered illegal.

Then it hit him. Of course, someone was trying to stop him scripting this biography. But who? And why? Keston felt cold; whoever it was had almost succeeded. Someone who wouldn't stop at murder . . . stubbornly, he decided that he was not going to be stopped.

After Flowers left to carry out his investigation, he recorded a report for Barnabas and sent it to Terra by messenger. He looked for the guide who had started the operation that saved his life and thanked him.

The Warden and Flowers returned to the terrace as he sat with a fresh drink.

'One of our waiters stetted out of here just before the hunt started,' the Warden said grimly. 'We found your seal in his room.'

Keston took it gratefully and slipped it back in his pocket. He was free to leave now, he thought, next stop Carnival — but first he had to get some protection. He went to the transmitting hall, and the operator dialled the co-ordinates he wanted.

But Keston was in too much of a hurry to get away, and forgot to take an anti-stetting pill. He stepped into the booth, into vertigo.

* * *

Jason Wainwright, Director-General of United Worlds, stood in full sunlight at a high window in UW Headquarters, staring gloomily out. He saw neither the sun, nor the long vista of city canyons reaching away from him; his mind was turned inward. The pervasive hum from the racks of computers in the long room at his back could not reach his thoughts.

His face was lined with harassment and the muscles of his hands twitched in sympathy with the problem tormenting him: it could come to war! For over a hundred years, United Worlds had been the power behind the Federation — a fact on which Terra's economy was based — maintaining a status quo between all the self-governing Earth-type planets. It had taken a long time for UW to gain acceptance from the majority — and that came with strings attached.

For instance, he thought, frowning, even with the situation as critical as it now was, he dare not contemplate direct police action; any force he sent to either Technos or Mogul would be taken as violation of the non-intervention pact. And the resulting uproar might well be the end of the Federation.

He sighed gustily, a solidly built man, nearing sixty, weighed down by his responsibilities. Economically, UW was dependent on subscriptions from each of the member worlds — and just how many of them would back him if he decided he *must* act? Yet the Federation had to be saved. Technos and Mogul could not be allowed to plunge the galaxy into war . . .

He felt that his hands were tied. Slowly, the city appeared to him as he came out of his reverie, and it seemed a place to get away from. Since his wife had died, he hardly ever left the treadmill between office and home.

A soft footfall on the rug behind him brought Wainwright swinging round. A slim young-looking man with a crisp wave in his prematurely grey hair held out a message form. 'From Park, sir.'

Wainwright smiled, shrugging off his worries, welcoming the triviality of the moment. He took the message from his deputy and glanced at it.

'So Barnabas was right after all. His man Keston really was in some danger. What d'you make of that, Neale?'

'Eden?' Neale suggested. 'He hasn't stirred from his world, despite the pleading of his supporters. If he's really planning to intervene, maybe he doesn't want his past dragged up.'

Wainwright considered the idea briefly. 'Could be, I suppose.' He didn't even like to think about Kyle Eden interfering; the balance was too delicate without that.

'Best set a watch on Keston,' he decided. 'See to it, will you?'

Neale nodded, and padded softly away.

Wainwright watched him go. He liked his new deputy. A bit young for the job, perhaps, but reliable. Highly competent. He didn't regret promoting him over the heads of others; Neale would be ready to take over when it was time for him to retire . . .

Back in his own office, Neale snapped on the communicator and gave quiet orders.

4

Copper

Hew Keston stumbled out of the stet booth on D'Amazone, his brain spinning like Saturn's rings, his stomach retching. He staggered across a black-and-white tiled floor, limbs made heavy and awkward by the increase in gravity, and groped for the rim of an ornamental drinking fountain in the centre of the hall.

He anchored himself to it, vomiting; swilled out his mouth and cursed himself for forgetting to take an anti-stetting pill. After a few minutes, the hall steadied around him and he drank; the water was cool and tasted of earth.

He began to feel better, straightened up and looked around; a robot cleaner was mopping up after him. The woman on duty at the reception desk viewed him with undisguised contempt. He tried out his legs and moved slowly towards her.

She was a rock of a woman, middle-aged, all bulges and craggy protuberances, formidable. Her voice had an edge to it. 'What do you want here?'

Keston, feeling almost half his weight again on this high-gravity world, sank carefully into a chair opposite her. 'I've come to hire a personal bodyguard — someone's trying to kill me.'

'How long do you want a guard?' she asked coolly. 'And do you have the necessary credit?'

Keston showed his seal, suppressing a shudder as he remembered Lomax; there would be no last minute reprieve for the hauler from Pedestar. 'I'm scripting a biography for Stereoscopics Inc. — I'll want protection for as long as the job takes.'

The receptionist checked his seal, looked him up and down, then nodded and pressed a button on her desk. They waited, ignoring each other.

Keston glanced at bare grey walls and an archway with a passage leading off; over the arch was a large sign: NO MAN PERMITTED BEYOND THIS POINT.

45

Only in the Federation, with freedom underwritten by UW, he thought, could such a matriarchy exist . . .

Presently, footsteps came clacking down the passage and across the tiled floor. The girl-warrior who answered the call was young and well-muscled. Short and stocky, she strode boldly on bare legs, head held high, arms swinging, confident. A laser handgun was holstered at the belt of her spartan tunic.

Keston heaved himself upright. Beneath short copper-coloured hair, wide tawny eyes glinted back at him from a square serious face. A head shorter than Keston, she still gave the impression of looking down at him as she gestured imperiously. 'Sit.'

'This is Adrienne,' the receptionist said. 'She will guard you.' A powerful hand thrust a plasti-metal contract form at him. 'Read this well before you seal it.'

Keston took the contract and a magnifier to read the microprint. There were clauses enough to keep a lawyer happy for a month, he thought sourly . . . but anyway, he had a general idea of the terms in advance.

D'Amazone guaranteed him full security while the contract lasted. His guard was licensed to kill in protection of her client. He skip-read his way through the major clauses, impressed his seal at the bottom and handed it back.

The receptionist deftly slid the flimsy plate into a pneumatic filing system and it vanished from view. She said calmly: 'Contract accepted. You're under our protection from this moment, Mr. Keston.'

He felt braver immediately. No one was going to stop him now. The women of D'Amazone were professionals, physically hardened by life on a high-gravity planet and instructed from birth in the arts of war. It was said they could kill with any weapon, or none; the whole economy of their world was based on the hiring out of bodyguards.

He looked appraisingly at the girl assuming responsibility for his life and thought her name, Adrienne, entirely unsuitable. Her hair, gleaming like copper wire, caught his eye and he said impulsively: 'I'm going to call you Copper.'

She shrugged, uninterested. 'We'll go to the guest chamber so you can give me the details of the assignment. See you later, Gwyneth.'

The receptionist nodded. Keston rose and followed the quick determined strides of his guard, panting with the effort to keep up; his experience on Park had not improved his physical shape all that much, he thought. Beyond another archway was a small doorless room with a plain table and two chairs.

'Do you need to eat?' Adrienne asked abruptly.

Feeling empty after his bout of stet-sickness, Keston nodded. 'Please . . .'

She raised her voice. A hatchway opened in the wall and two brawny arms thrust a loaded tray, holding two plates of almost raw meat and two glasses of water, through the gap. Keston found himself wondering what the quarters were like beyond the point where no men were allowed. It made for intriguing speculation.

Adrienne handed Keston her knife and began to pull her own steak apart with her fingers. 'Now,' she commanded, 'tell me.'

Between leathery mouthfuls, he said: 'I'm a scripter, working on a biography of the Edens — '

Keston saw her tense at the name, and cursed his thoughtlessness. Of course, she would have no time for the Eden legend, based as it was on a heredity descent from son to son. The women of D'Amazone despised men and had nothing to do with them; they propagated their race by artificial insemination, buying frozen semen from other worlds.

'Mythical nonsense,' she said curtly.

Keston hurried on: 'Anyway, somebody tried to kill me on Park, I suspect to try to stop me completing the job.' He told her about the man who had been watching him on Terra, and the waiter who had switched his seal. 'So I thought I'd hire some protection,' he ended.

Adrienne nodded, thoughtful. 'You do whatever it is you have to do in your job

49

— I'll just tag along and see you stay alive to do it.'

Keston pushed his half-finished meal aside, vaguely irritated by her manner. It was too superior, he decided, far too superior — but then he was dealing with women who had set out to prove men wholly unnecessary. 'Let's go,' he snapped, 'I want to visit Carnival next.'

They returned to the hall, and Gwyneth set the dials on a booth. Keston remembered to swallow an anti-stetting pill. Then, with his bodyguard beside him, he stepped through . . .

Multi-coloured lights blazed in the sky. A fanfare of music rolled over him. The reception area was outdoors and seemed to be filled with balloons and streamers and people wearing fancy dress and masks. A speaking system brayed from among lanterns hung in the trees:

'Welcome to Carnival, the brightest spot in the galaxy! Get our costume and mask and join in the fun!'

Keston signed in, turning down the offer of a red-and-yellow check suit; he was here to work. Adrienne kept a pace to his rear. Gravity on Carnival was slightly less than on Terra, giving Keston the feeling he was bouncing along; it meant that Copper would move even faster if it became necessary.

He hired a helicab to take them to Eden's Joyhouse. The cab whirred away above a torch-lit procession of fantastic floats, over several acres of fairground, past an island with a white dome and flashing neon: CASINO.

The cab descended slowly onto a landing platform beside a glittering folly of a building that sprawled across a green landscape; gothic towers vied with a modern sun lounge, pagodas and minarets with tiers of cube-shaped cabins that rose like giant stepping stones to a spherical penthouse. Over the years, a series of architects had built extensions onto the original joyhouse, so that the result looked as if a madman had planned it.

A tout pounced on Keston the moment he stepped from the cab onto springy turf. 'A conducted tour of the most famous pleasure establishment in the galaxy, sir. Only seventy-five credits! Everything goes on Carnival — you want girls? We've got them, all shapes, colours and specialities. You want drugs to weave your own individual fantasy? We've got narcotics from every known planet in the Federation! If you want — '

Amused, Keston walked past him. 'I want the manager,' he said, and sat down at a table beneath exotic Chinese lanterns. Eden had been a tout, too, he remembered.

He ordered *Old Rye* for himself and looked questioningly at Adrienne. Her lips set in a line of disapproval. 'Alcohol will ruin your reaction time,' she told him flatly.

It was evening on Carnival, but the night sky was obscured by a blaze of light. Music blared and men and women from a hundred different worlds danced in bizarre costumes and masks. Hostesses, naked except for a few glittering jewels, moved between the tables.

Keston fidgeted, glanced sideways at Adrienne; without her, he could have enjoyed himself here. He felt too embarrassed to look openly at the hostesses while she sat beside him, her expression scarcely concealing her contempt for their display of feminine charms.

A loudspeaker announced: 'The finalists in the Miss Eden contest will parade now!'

As he sat drinking, watching the masked dancers, Keston began to feel uneasy. The thought occurred to him that, with everyone wearing masks, an assassin could easily creep up on him.

Adrienne appeared to read his mind. 'Relax, Mr. Keston — you don't have to worry while I'm here.' She seemed to be enjoying the situation. 'These glamour girls may please your eye, but do you think they could take care of you as well as I can?'

He returned his attention to the beauty contestants; at least they were wearing clothes, high-necked and ground-sweeping, in contrast to the hostesses. He could view them without embarrassment. They paraded in a long line before him, mounting a dais where the judges sat, handpicked beauties from all the worlds of the Federation. He was mentally picking the winner — a long-legged girl from Sunstar IV — when the manager stepped up to his table.

The sleek manicured figure was visibly jolted by the sight of Keston's companion. But he recovered quickly and said: 'You wish some special service, sir?'

'I'm scripting for Stereoscopic, hunting material on the Eden clan.'

'Then you've come to the right place, sir.' The manager snapped his fingers and a hostess glided up with a bulky directory. 'Eden was born here, sir. His mother was a hostess. At fourteen, he began work as a guide — '

For guide, read tout, Keston thought, flipping coloured pages. 'This is just the usual handout — what I'm looking for are facts, names, dates, stuff that can be cross-checked.'

The manager assumed a poker expression. 'It was so long ago, sir. I doubt very much if — '

'Surely there must be somebody interested in the old days?' Keston persisted.

The manager's eyes lighted, as if inspired. 'Well, there's our Fool, of course — he fancies himself as an amateur historian, though publicity says he can't always be trusted. He might have something you can use. I'll fix you an interview with him for tomorrow . . . Stereoscopic will give us a mention, naturally?'

'Naturally,' Keston assured him.

The manager bowed and left. Keston finished his drink and went to book adjoining rooms for the night.

His feet sank into thick pile as he entered the joyhouse; perfumed air stirred gently; a smiling hostess approached him. Keston looked at her and looked away, giving a brusque shake of his head. He walked on, his breath coming quickly.

Adrienne smiled tolerantly. 'Don't mind me, Mr. Keston. This isn't my first assignment — I've seen it all before.'

Keston scowled as they stepped into the lift together. The cage rose, stopped, and the gate opened automatically. Adrienne stepped out first, hand on gun-butt; she moved ahead to check the room.

Inside an illuminated sign winked: 'Visit the erotic penthouse for a night of strange delights!'

Adrienne smirked. 'Going to try it?'

Keston refused to reply. He removed the top half of his casuals and stepped into the bathroom. He was about to slide the door shut when Adrienne stopped him.

'Now look, Copper,' he said wearily. 'I know that a guard has to stick close to her client, but I need some privacy. Like now, for instance.'

'No,' she said calmly, 'No privacy. It was in the contract, if you'd bothered to read it carefully. I don't leave you, not for a moment, not for any reason.'

Keston glared at her, helpless to disagree. He needed protection, but he wasn't going to like getting used to this kind of surveillance . . . Copper was definitely going to be something of an embarrassment, he decided, taking a perfunctory wash. It would help if she'd stop grinning like a nursemaid with a small boy.

He returned to the bedroom; it was a huge double bed of the old-fashioned kind, designed for pleasure-lovers. He looked at it, then at his bodyguard. 'I booked the adjoining room for you,' he hinted.

She ignored the hint with a shake of her copper head, loosened her tunic and stretched out on the floor across the doorway, gun in hand. 'You can put the light out if you're shy.'

Fuming, Keston ripped off the rest of his garment and climbed into bed.

'Sleep tight,' Adrienne called mockingly. 'Pleasant dreams!'

Keston scowled up at the mirror set in the ceiling above him. Acutely conscious of her lying there on the floor, he waited a long time for sleep to come.

5

Riddle Me Ree

He woke abruptly, soaked in sweat, the piercing blast of a hunting horn ringing in his head. Struggling up from under a tangle of silken sheets, Keston saw Adrienne, awake and watching him with mockery in her tawny eyes, and felt foolish. 'Only a dream,' he croaked.

But the dream had nightmarish qualities and he shuddered as its echoes washed over him: he had been hunted through a strange shifting landscape by giant-sized girl warriors, led by Copper. And every time she triggered her gun, derisive laughter boomed from the bell-shaped muzzle. He was glad the night was over.

He washed, depilated, and dressed under her casual gaze; still somewhat embarrassed but feeling better, he descended to the dining room. Adrienne demanded meat for breakfast, plenty of it and near-raw. Keston dined off some exotic dish he could not recognize but tasted a whole lot better than Terra's staple, soya steak.

As he lingered over coffee, a bejewelled hostess swayed up to his table and smiled at him. 'If you will follow me, sir, I'll conduct you to the Fool.'

Keston rose and followed her, mentally comparing the hostess's soft and feminine figure with the sturdy muscular frame of his bodyguard. Adrienne seemed to know what was in his mind, and murmured: 'She's the kind men go for, isn't she? So why pretend you're not looking at her?'

Keston averted his gaze from his guide's rear end. They passed through a hall where early-morning gamblers were engrossed in row upon row of slot machines; levers rachetted, coloured marbles rattled along pin-tracks — and sometimes prize-winning discs showered from a chute. None of the players looked up as they passed; totally absorbed, they might have been cyborgs permanently attached to their machines.

Behind the Aqua-Shop and a queue outside the soothsayer's pad — 'THREE SHIFTS WORKING, NO WAITING' — they went down a sloping tunnel to a wood-panelled door. The hostess knocked and opened it, left them with a smile.

Keston stepped into a small room crammed with bookshelves; a camp bed, table and chair were not merely old, but old-fashioned. A wiry man with white hair and flushed cheeks was struggling into a parti-coloured costume.

'You're Keston, I suppose?' the Fool grunted. 'And a guard too, eh? You want to know all about Eden . . . come in, come in and shut the door.'

The old man smoothed out the wrinkles in his costume and sat down heavily. His voice ran on as if he were used to talking to himself.

'The legend isn't good enough for you, is that it?' Not many want the truth, but you do. Don't tell me why. I don't want to know. But you've come to the right man . . .

'Listen, Keston, my family were Fools here in the time of Alain and it's been handed down, word of mouth, you understand. But I'll give you the truth as I remember it, can't say fairer than that, can I? A Fool can say anything to anybody and no harm done, no one listens, no one takes any notice any more . . . Sad really.

'We have a long history, you know, began on Terra — originally a religious function. In those days the King had absolute power, directly given him by the Gods. Anyone argue with the king, off with his head! Except the Fool — he was the only man who could tell the King he was wrong. A useful — '

'About Eden,' Keston interrupted gently, switching on his mini-recorder.

'Yes, yes, I'm coming to him, don't rush me,' the old man said testily. 'He was nothing, a nobody, always poor, always hungry . . . the joyhouse wasn't as you see it today. They cashed in on his name when he became a legend.'

Adrienne leaned against the door, bored. She had no interest in Eden, or any other man.

'Alain swore he'd be rich one day,

powerful, with the best of everything,' the Fool said. 'It became an obsession with him . . . you want to know how he got that rep job on Park?

'He bought it, bought it with stolen money. Alain Eden was a common thief, they don't put that in the legend, do they? Publicity wouldn't like it, but that's how it was. He skipped with a girl and the joyhouse takings . . . and they couldn't do a thing about it, didn't even know where he'd gone till long after.'

Keston thought: So there *was* a girl, after all

'He bought the rep's job. Oh, he was smart all right, he could see the laser handgun was worth something. That's how it started; he went on and on and never looked back. Well, maybe once . . . d'you ever hear of the Junkworld? That doesn't get much of a mention either in the history records. He was still a rep, even then, this time for a new everlasting plastic, but things went wrong and he got into trouble with the law.

'You'll find it all set down in the courthouse records, I dare say. But nobody bothers, nobody goes there any more . . . it's one of the derelict worlds.'

The Fool put on his coxcomb and picked up his staff; his eyes sparked with malicious glee. 'I'll set you three riddles, Keston, three riddles to solve so you'll start thinking for yourself and forget all this legendary crap.' He paused and took a long breath. 'The first is this: *Why is Eden's face like a pea in a pod?* That's an easy one . . .

'Now for my second riddle, and this is: *Which came first, Eden or his Beast?* Not so easy, Keston? Third and last, then: *If Eden's World is dark as night, why is it there's no wandering light?* Riddle me, riddle me ree!'

The old man cackled with laughter and waved Adrienne away from the door. 'A Fool's work is never done,' he said as he opened it and went out.

Adrienne sniffed, 'A crackpot if I ever met one.'

Keston ignored her, shutting off his recorder, listening to footsteps fade in the passage, thinking . . .

Peas in a pod were all the same, or said

to be. Alain, Morg, David and Kyle — the image had been standardized of course. The face was the same, handsome with a generous hint of nobility, the hero of stereo. He racked his brain for another picture, but his memory refused to come up with any different version of the legendary Eden. And that was a little strange, come to think of it . . .

The Beast. Had Eden always had the beast? No, not in the early legends; there was no mention of it there. Somewhere on his travels then, he'd met it. But where? And when?

Eden's World was no part of the Federation, no Earth-type planet, but a sunless wanderer, permanently dark and heated by its own internal fires. Where had it come from? And why had the Edens claimed it for their own?

Keston realized that the Fool's riddles had set him thinking the way he should have been thinking before. He had to go behind the legend. He didn't know nearly enough about either the origins of the Beast or Eden's strange world.

He left the Fool's room and hurried

back up the tunnel, excited: stet to the Junkworld first, he thought — check the court records, there should be a useful lead there.

Adrienne, padding along cat-like at his back, mocked: 'Set a Fool to catch a thief! Riddles yet.'

Outside the tunnel, Keston paused at a stereo screen as a news bulletin flashed on:

'Deterling of Mogul has issued a new proclamation! In it, he states emphatically that Mogul desires only a peaceful expansion with those worlds willing to come under his banner. He further states that, if war comes, it will be only because Technos has illegally interfered in the plans of Mogul!'

★ ★ ★

Deterling of Mogul stood stiffly at attention on a high dais amid waving banners, clad in a black military uniform. Behind his broad back, the walls of the fortress, grim and forbidding, towered high into a cloudy sky. Watery patches of

65

sunlight played a shifting pattern across his bald gorilla skull; and his gaze roved over the ranks of black uniforms marching past in review.

As he took the salute from his nobles and their armies, he thought: more men plus more guns equalled more taxes, and his mouth curved in a cruel smile. A man who had gained power by cunning and treachery, he knew how to handle any malcontents.

The fortress stood high on a hill, its towers buttressed by dark rock, above the small town and commanding a long view across the patchwork green-and-brown fields to the river beyond.

Mogul was a feudal world, divided up into fiefs, each with its own lord who owed allegiance to Deterling; tenure was held by military service, rent payable in steel. It was a system that suited him, and he was prepared to go to any length to maintain it; certain nobles who had once had the idea of replacing him were swiftly murdered and their heads mounted on poles outside the fortress. The weathered skulls rested there yet as a warning to others.

Attaining mastery of one planet had given him the taste for power, and he craved more. His gaze turned outward, to the many backward worlds of the Federation. Now, all his energies were directed to building up his armies . . .

Only Redmont of Technos threatened his plans for expansion; and Deterling's spies reported that Redmont was readying to move — so he must strike first, and hard, or have a major war on his hands. He could not afford that; it was easy pickings that Deterling sought. A scowl creased his fleshy face as he brooded over it. Technos had superiority in technicians and weapons — but he had the advantage in manpower. Strike first, and Redmont would be overwhelmed.

His attack on Freedom would be a test case, to see if the opposition amounted to anything.

At his back, an aide hurried up to whisper in his ear: 'The communicator, sire.'

Deterling stepped down from the dais and hastened back to the portable communicator set shielded from the casual gaze by a canvas awning. No picture showed on the screen, but he knew the voice well enough:

'Keston has arrived on Carnival, accompanied by a guard of D'Amazone. He is asking about Eden — '

Deterling stiffened, forced a blank mask over his face. Curse the Edens . . . others might doubt the truth of legend, but he believed. A family who had achieved all that the Edens had could not be easily discounted.

United Worlds would not stop him. Deterling despised the Terran organization; moreover he had his own plans for handling Wainwright. Redmont wouldn't bother him either if he moved fast . . . but Eden? What was *he* up to?

The voice from the dead screen asked a question. Deterling considered; he had no liking for this man, but he needed him — for the moment. He snapped an order and switched off the set, turned back to the review.

From the dais, he stared unseeing at the massed ranks marching past, saluted absently. Men and weapons. Yet, his mind on Kyle Eden, he felt uneasy; he worried, feeling the need for a diversion.

Turning the review over to one of his nobles, he entered the fortress. The stone corridors were gloomy with shadows; a guard saluted as he stepped into his private apartment. Rich drapes hung from the walls; his throne glittered; a silken couch waited.

A servant poured him a drink and he gulped it down in one mouthful. He lit an imported cigar, the best; but in his mood it tasted foul and he stubbed it out almost immediately. There were dark shadows in the room . . . damned sun-power lamps never worked properly on cloudy days.

Outside, a drumbeat started up, slow, monotonous. *Vroom-vroom! Vroom, vroom, vroom!*

He began to pace the stone floor, glanced at the couch and lifted his voice to a shout: 'Bring me a woman! Magda, that black-haired wench!'

6

Death on Junkworld

Keston stepped out of a stet booth on Junkworld. The reception centre was dusty from disuse and moulds spawned in neglected corners.

Adrienne's nose wrinkled in disgust. 'It's dirty — and smelly!'

The man at the desk was as grey and gloomy as his surroundings. Surprise flickered in his faded eyes. He opened the logbook to a fresh page and inscribed the year at the top. 'You're the first visitors we've had for a long time,' he said dolefully. 'Tourists? Perhaps people are beginning to remember us again.'

Keston impressed his seal and asked the way to the courthouse.

'Down the street, sir. The new building. You can't miss it — it's the only new building hereabouts.'

Keston walked outside. A wind keened

along the deserted street, dusting it with fine grey powder, blurring the outline of derelict houses and walls already collapsed. The slum area seemed to extend right through the town, to the horizon; and beyond, towered slag heaps of plastic junk, conglomerations of containers of all shapes and sizes, cans, bottles, cartons.

The sky appeared as listless as the land, barren of life. Adrienne padded silently along behind Keston as he walked amid a litter of rubbish in a world where nothing grew any more, a dust bowl of discarded plastic forms. The Junkworld was a dead-end, ugly and depressing.

Among the heaps of debris, Keston glimpsed a few men and women, thin and shabbily dressed, scavengers who existed by breaking down the plastic discards and converting them to sell cheaply on some other world. He saw no children. The youngsters had gone elsewhere to make their living — this was a dying planet, a graveyard for inanimate objects.

Keston walked hurriedly, trying to hold his breath to avoid the all-pervading smell of decay. He passed the ruins of a building with faded letters on its façade: ANTI-EDEN LEAGUE — H.Q. A few *I Hate Eden* badges lay in the dust, and he stooped and picked one up, pinned it on. Something told him that was likely to be an open-sesame here.

The courthouse was new only in comparison with the rest of the town; already it had begun to take on a neglected air. The windows were grey, the steps dust-coated. He pushed open a creaking door.

Inside, the custodian resembled a scarecrow with rheumy eyes and threadbare dress.

Keston said: 'I'm scripting a biography of Eden — '

Hatred flared briefly in the old man's eyes and died away. 'Don't mention that name here . . . lies, all lies, all of it. The legend is — '

'I'm here to get the facts,' Keston said firmly. 'I'm not interested in legends. I want the truth, what really happened. And it'll go out over Stereo.'

The custodian's lips twisted in a bitter smile. 'And who will believe it? The legend has a stranglehold now. Eden is a hero . . . a pox on him! He came here, you know, as a trader's rep for a new kind of plastic. Everlasting plastic, it was called — sold as indestructible. Unfortunately for us — ' He gestured vaguely at the mountains of junk encroaching on the town limits — 'Unfortunately the name is all too true. It lived up to its publicity. We still can't get rid of it, those few of us left.

'In the early days, our people were opening up a new world, and this plastic seemed a good thing to exploit. We set up automated factories to produce it, filled the planet to overflowing. Then we found that we couldn't sell all we produced and it piled up and began to choke the streets. It killed off the vegetation.'

Keston, recorder switched on, listened, nodding.

'Other worlds realized we had a tiger by the tail and wouldn't buy any more. We were stuck with it. Then the hatred began, and the riots — some were for lynching Eden if they could find him. He was hiding out under a false name. He was a criminal, you hear me, a criminal . . . he ruined a whole world!'

Adrienne looked at Keston, mocking. 'What price your hero now?' she murmured.

Keston ignored her.

The custodian went on: 'At that time, United Worlds had just got going. This was one of their first policing actions — they arrested Eden and brought him to trial. Guilty as he was, he pleaded good intentions — and got off with banishment. He got off too light — he should have hung! Some said he bribed UW . . .

'But the people here were still stuck with this everlasting plastic. There was just no way of getting rid of it — the stuff simply won't wear out. Then the young folk started to leave, a whole world emptied. It's derelict now, apart from a few scavengers. The Junkworld!'

Keston waited patiently, but the custodian remained silent, like a clockwork doll run down. 'Was Eden alone when he came? Or was there a girl with him? Or his Beast?'

The custodian scratched his head. 'Alone, so far as I remember the story. No girl. This was before the Beast.'

'The records of the trial — can I view them?'

'No sir, you cannot! Soon after the trial, the courthouse burnt down. Perhaps it was the mob, angry at being thwarted; perhaps Eden himself, covering his past. All the records burnt with it. This is a new building.'

Keston turned away, disappointed. His lead seemed to have petered out, So it was only hearsay, as yet — his mouth set stubbornly — but somewhere, somehow, he would track the story down.

Adrienne's feet shifted impatiently. 'Where to now? Somewhere that smells better, I hope.'

Keston stepped out onto the street, stared over the tumbledown houses to the mountains looming on every horizon; artificial mountains, tremendous slagheaps of plastic junk. He started walking; maybe he should question a few of the scavengers while he was here?

Adrienne suddenly gave him a violent shove in the small of his back, sending him sprawling in the dirt. 'Stay down!'

she yelled. Keston mumbled, startled: 'What do you — '

There was a terrifying hiss as a rocket-propelled barb skittered over his head and ricocheted off the ground and hit a wall further on. Its explosive head shattered and the blast picked up Keston and carried him along the street.

He hit the ground again, and lay still, badly frightened. Through falling dust he saw the flash of a hand-laser. *Copper!* A small figure tumbled from a window to the street. It did not move again.

Keston hugged the ground, watching the girl warrior. Legs braced, she stood like a rock, gun poised, scanning the street. A second man darted out holding an electro-knife.

Adrienne moved to face him, holstered her gun with quiet confidence and grappled as he closed in. For a long moment they struggled against each other, muscles tensed and straining, then her hands wrapped around his neck and bone snapped.

Keston heard it snap — distinctly — and shuddered.

She dropped the limp body and, hand on gun-butt, looked round. 'All right, Mr. Keston — ' There was amusement in her voice — 'You can get up now. These two are just so much more junk.'

Keston rose slowly, breathless and covered in dust. Fear made his legs weak; his hands shook as he brushed himself down.

Adrienne turned both bodies face-up with her foot. 'Recognize either of them?' she asked.

Keston stared at the blank faces and, voiceless, shook his head.

Deftly, she turned out their pockets. 'No papers, no identi-seals. Professionals, hired for the job — and I doubt if we'll trace the hirer. It looks as if somebody wants you dead.'

'I knew that already,' Keston croaked, finding his voice.

The custodian came out to gawk at the corpses. A few scavengers gathered round. It was the first excitement any of them could remember on the Junkworld. 'There'll have to be a trial,' the custodian said, eager to prolong the moment.

Adrienne turned on him, at her most imperious. 'I am a guard of D'Amazone!'

'But we must have a trial — '

Keston began to fret. He wanted off the Junkworld, but not without Copper. He wasn't going anywhere without his bodyguard, not now . . . unbidden, the second of the Fool's riddles danced through his brain: *Which came first, Eden or his Beast?*

He turned to the custodian, and asked: 'D'you have a data input here?'

'In the courthouse.'

Keston retraced his steps to the courthouse and located the operating board of the information centre. He punched buttons and a screen lit up, showing a picture of the Beast, with Eden in the saddle, trotting through park-like gardens set between tall buildings. He studied it carefully; as tall and heavy as a workhorse, a pale grey in colour, its single horn — straight and tapering to a sharp point, about a foot long — projected from between its eyes. There was no doubt the Beast was an animal, and not a robot faked up.

'The Beast of Eden,' intoned a mechanical voice, 'the only one known of its kind in the galaxy. Alien; origin unknown, but not native to any G-type planet. First made its appearance shortly before the marriage of Alain Eden to the Lady Sin of Mathematica. Under infra-red light, a faint but distinct aura of radiation is visible. Requests for further investigation and information were refused by the Edens.'

Keston switched off. The first Eden, he thought, and decided where he was going next. Honeymoon; there would be records there . . . He wondered what had happened to the hostess Eden had ditched somewhere.

The custodian was still harrying Copper. 'You must wait — I insist! A United Worlds agent will be here shortly.'

Keston stood in the doorway, looking down the street, Adrienne said: 'Ready to leave now?'

A thickset figure with iron-grey hair and wearing uniform hurried from the direction of the stet station. *Flowers*! Keston stared blankly at the man from

Park. 'What are you doing here?'

The UW agent ignored the question, looked at Adrienne. 'Your identification, please,' he said briskly.

Flowers studied her identi-seal, handed it back and listened as she told her story. When she had finished, he glanced at Keston. 'You'll want to move soon, I expect?'

Keston nodded, and Flowers faced the Junkworlders. He listened patiently as first one, then another, gave their versions. Finally, he lifted his hand and rattled off the customary formula:

'By the authority vested in me by United Worlds, the trial of Adrienne of D'Amazone, accused of killing two unknown men on the Junkworld, is now in session. The defendant claims that she killed in defence of her client, Hew Keston of Terra. No evidence to the contrary has been shown. The court therefore accepts the defendant's plea. Case dismissed.'

Keston looked gratefully at Flowers. 'Many thanks . . . er, would UW have records of the trial of Alain Eden? The trial that was held here.'

Flowers shrugged. 'It's possible — you'd have to go to Terran H.Q. to find out.'

'Some other time then.' Keston took Copper's arm and started down the road to the stet station, wondering how the UW man happened to be on the spot so quickly.

★   ★   ★

Redmont, Autarch of Technos, sat watching a wall-sized stereo screen; roving camera eyes brought him a world of spotless cities, anthills swarming with busy technicians.

A humourless smile creased his thin ascetic face. A tall man with dark grey eyes, he stared at the changing panorama — constantly changing yet always the same — and reflected that he had created the best of all possible worlds. He suppressed a rising glow of satisfaction. There was still room for improvement. Technology was the answer, the only answer; a thriving world, adequate food, separate apartments, an expanding economy.

Expanding. That was the key word. His bloodless lips pressed firmly together as he recalled United Worlds. Any fool could see he had the answer and that it must be put into effect on all Federation planets. Yet the UW charter expressly forbade any kind of interference.

Not for much longer, he decided. He admitted that UW had served a purpose earlier — Technos itself might have been overrun by some barbarian horde — but those days were past. UW had to go.

The time had come for a strong Technos to take the poorer worlds into its fold and help them rise. Redmont was sure he knew what was best for them . . . for a moment, the light of fanaticism gleamed in his eyes. Technology was more than science; it was a religion to him.

His thoughts turned to Deterling. He had no more than contempt for the man; a latter-day imitation of Jenghiz Khan. But Mogul had soldiers, hordes of them. So Technos must forestall his attempt to build an empire.

A strident buzzing filled the room.

Redmont pressed a button at the side of his chair and the view of the planet faded from the screen, to be replaced by the head and shoulders of an overalled Communications Technician.

'Reverend Autarch: from Intelligence. A Terran scripter, Hew Keston by name, is stetting round the Federation worlds, gathering material for a new biography of the Eden Clan. It is considered that Kyle Eden may have instigated this himself, through the operator, Barnabas . . . '

Redmont's high forehead wrinkled in concentration. Quinn, his Chief of Intelligence, would not be bothering him with this at the moment they were planning the invasion of Botan unless . . .

Eden. Always, at the back of his mind, had been the idea that Kyle Eden might try to interfere in his plans for the galaxy. Was this the first move by that recluse forever brooding on his sunless wanderer?

Redmont stroked his jaw, deliberating. He had no tine for legends; but he could make use of Eden. Yes, he could certainly do that. Keston would only be a pawn; yet the taking of a pawn could affect the whole outcome of a game. His gaze flicked to the man in the screen: 'Tell Quinn to find this Keston for me.'

He sat thinking a while, and then pushed another button on his chair. 'Send Venner to me.' Venner should take care of Mogul for the moment.

He considered again, and called Research. 'Is the new machine ready yet?'

'Almost, Reverend Autarch . . . '

'Prepare it for immediate operation!'

Redmont of Technos smiled coldly as he meditated on his counter-moves.

7

Gone missing

Keston arrived on Honeymoon at a busy time. The hall was large and crowded with smiling couples; the air warm and everyone lightly clad. There was a scent of blossoms and a hubbub of gaiety. Young marrieds from two score Federation worlds formed a queue at the reception desk, and Keston and Adrienne joined on at the end.

Honeymoon was the tourist planet for newly-weds, and posters on the walls — in delicate pastel shades — showed tri-D views of secluded nooks and romantic beaches. A large sign proclaimed: *Exclusively robot service — YOU ARE ALONE AT ALL TIMES*.

Eventually, Keston reached the desk and produced his seal. The clerk said, automatically: 'Formalities, sir and madame. Your names, please — home worlds — marriage certificates.'

Keston almost burst out laughing . . . a guard of D'Amazone marrying! He held his laughter in check as he replied: 'We're not married. I'm here on business, and this is my guard.'

The clerk looked at them, dumbfounded. 'But we've only married quarters — '

'They'll do,' Keston said drily. Since Copper had saved his life on the Junkworld, his attitude towards her had changed; he no longer wanted to be separated from her. 'I just want to check an item with your records section.'

'Tomorrow, please,' the harassed clerk begged. 'We really are rushed.'

Keston agreed to wait, and an automated hovercar drove them to their cabin, intoning: 'Happiness, sir and madame.'

The cabin, a typical Honeymoon prefab unit, was small, shaded by trees, with an alien flower resembling a rose growing on a trellis round the door. Inside a pneumatic double bed took up most of the floor space. A control panel, studded with pushbuttons, was labeled: *Service*.

The walls were covered with advertising matter that contrasted strangely with the romantic posters in reception:

TRY SEXI FOR THAT EXTRA BOOST
BETTER TAKE ANTIMATE —
THE SAFEST SAFEGUARD

Adrienne laughed. 'All wasted on us, I'm afraid . . . still, you can always come back!'

Keston punched buttons and a meal was served. Afterwards, he strolled outside. A gentle breeze stirred the leaves and brought a fragrant scent. It was quiet. It seemed he was quite alone under three small moons that gave a shifting pattern of silver light.

He moved casually through the shadows. Honeymoon really was the most romantic place in the galaxy, he thought, the perfect setting for love. For a moment, he envied the young couples he'd seen arriving . . .

Behind him, Adrienne's voice broke in harshly: 'Trying to make a target of yourself?'

Keston retreated hastily to the cabin

and locked the door. He had forgotten the fear he knew on the Junkworld; that was the measure of security he felt in being with Copper. Without his earlier sense of embarrassment, he undressed and went to bed.

After breakfast, a hovercraft drove them to the records section, intoning: 'Happiness, sir and madame.' They passed sunny glades and arbors where loving honeymooners sported, arriving at a circular building of tinted stone and glass.

The archivist, brisk and sure of himself, advanced to greet them. 'What can I do for you?'

Keston introduced himself and explained what he wanted.

'Alain Eden . . . dear me, that was a long time ago. Still, I expect we can find something for you.' The archivist looked slyly at Keston. 'Not exactly the place for work, eh? Follow me, please.'

They passed through a long room with fluorescent walls where computers pulsed, down a long corridor to underground vaults. The archivist began a methodical search.

Presently, he pulled out a bundle of records and blew the dust off them. 'This was before we fitted the latest computers,' he explained. 'Still . . . '

Keston waited eagerly.

'Ah, here's something now . . . Alain Eden arrived for a honeymoon trip with the Lady Sin of Mathematica, accompanied by his beast. They stayed six months . . . h'm, an unusually long time . . . ah, I see that a son, Morg, was born to them here.'

Keston nodded thoughtfully. It had been bothering him how Eden — with his past — had married into one of the most aristocratic families of Mathematica, itself a more than somewhat exclusive world. It looked as if he'd had to.

Morg. Son of the first Eden, the true start of the Eden clan that spanned more than a century.

The archivist continued to turn papers, reading. 'There's not much more, I'm afraid — a brief note informing that the Lady Sin died in space shortly after leaving here. But then the Edens always had bad luck in that direction, didn't they? Always the mother dying after the firstborn son . . . '

An idea pricked at Keston's scalp, and he asked: 'There'll be a medical record, of course?'

'Of course. Compulsory, you know.' The archivist began another search. He frowned. 'There doesn't seem to be . . . but there must be!' He grew dusty and impatient, as he searched and finally admitted defeat. 'This is most irregular, but it seems I must report the medical record is missing.'

Keston had somehow expected it, and exchanged a glance with Copper. The courthouse on the Junkworld had burnt down; now a medical record missing. He wondered: for the same reason and by the same hand?

He thanked the archivist and slowly retraced his steps to the surface. The beast had been with Eden. Was that significant? He wanted to know where Eden had met the beast — and the Lady Sin.

At the exit hall of the records section, a robot was paging: 'Hew Keston of Terra.

Stet message for Hew Keston of Terra.'

He identified himself and, almost immediately, a stet messenger in scarlet and grey uniform appeared. Keston showed his seal and impressed the logbook, ripped open the plastiform to read:

Keston. I have arranged an interview for you with Kyle Eden. Make your own way to Eden's world at the earliest possible moment. Barnabas.

Keston whistled incredulously. So Barnabas had swung it; he couldn't guess how, but he had an interview with the last of the clan. That was really something.

'Any answer?' the stet messenger asked.

Keston shook his head and the messenger saluted and left. There remained only the problem of getting there. It was well known that Eden did not have a stet booth on his own wandering planet. So stet to the nearest world — whichever was nearest at the moment — and then . . .

A hovercar intoning 'Happiness, sir and madame,' carried them to the departure centre, where Keston put his problem to the duty operator.

'The nearest planet to Eden's world, sir?' The operator checked the star tables. 'That'll be Neoism.' He crossed to a vacant booth and adjusted the dials. Checking casually, he said: 'I'm an Eden man myself. Yessir, Kyle'll sure enough step in and stop this war, you can bet on that. Like Eden says, 'The right man, in the right place, at the right time, is everything!' As Technos and Mogul will find out . . . ready when you are, sir.'

Keston put an anti-stetting pill on his tongue and swallowed. With Adrienne, he stepped into the booth; the holster of her laser gun dug into his side, reassuring him.

The door slid smoothly shut. A wink of an eye, he thought, and they'd —

Seconds dragged by. The light went out. And stayed out.

'What's happening?' Keston croaked, fear shivering along his spine. He clutched Copper's arm. 'What's gone wrong?'

In the blackness, he sensed her draw her gun.

Time seemed to stand still. Then the light came on and he saw a figure beyond the glass panelling; but still the door did not open. He began to choke.

'Something's wrong with the air . . . '

'Hold your breath!' Adrienne hissed.

It was too late for that. His legs buckled under him. His head swam. Gas, he thought wildly . . . they'd got him after all . . . and wondered who *they* were.

He slid slowly on the floor, losing consciousness. His last image was of Copper standing guard over him, grim-faced from holding her breath, blasting a shot through the glass door of the booth.

Then — *nothing*.

★   ★   ★

Wainwright pushed a pile of papers — reports, requests, suggestions — to one side and drummed stubby fingers on the desktop. His brooding gaze went to the racks of computers humming in the background. Feed in data; get back a choice of alternative solutions, but still he, as Director-General, had to make the final decision.

Lines etched his face; his expression was grave. Field reports no longer left him with the slightest doubt that both Mogul and Technos were determined on expansion — and that they were bound to clash, with the inevitable result of galactic war.

Wainwright shivered. So far, wars had always been planetary, but now . . . unless United Worlds stepped in first, breaking the charter. That would be the end of UW, and the Federation. He sighed heavily. He felt he would like to resign . . .

Neale, his deputy, pushed through a glass swing door into the room, padding softly towards him, a message form in one hand and a worried expression overriding his young-looking face.

Wainwright watched him come. The son he'd wanted and never had would be Neale's age now. 'What is it?' he asked.

Neale sounded puzzled. 'A stet message from Flowers, sir. About Keston, remember?'

Wainwright remembered. Keston —

Eden. All he wanted now to complete the agony was interference by Kyle Eden. He grimaced as he took the message form and read it through. It jolted him. When he came to the end, he read it again, slowly.

From Field Agent Flowers
To UW HQ, Terra:
'Keston left Honeymoon via stet for Neoism, which is now the closest planet to Eden's World. As instructed, I followed to keep him under observation. On Neoism, I was told that neither he nor his D'Amazone guard had arrived there; further investigation confirmed this report. I returned to Honeymoon and checked with their departure centres. Keston and his guard were correctly logged out — co-ordinates check — and the duty operator is positive that they left together. A volunteer tested the booth; result, no detectable fault. I have placed the booth out of service until our own experts can examine it. Meanwhile, Keston has disappeared. I

await further orders.'

Wainwright stared blankly at Neale. 'Disappeared? How could he disappear? What does it mean?'

Neale shrugged uneasily. 'I suppose stet could have broken down temporarily.'

'And suppose it didn't.' Wainwright did not complete his thought in speech. He rose and went to the window, his back to Neale, staring down into the concrete canyons of Terra's greatest city. 'I don't like the sound of it,' he said. 'I don't like the sound of this at all.'

Neale waited a long moment before asking: 'What orders for Flowers, sir?'

Wainwright ignored the question. He began to pace. 'Suppose — just suppose — that someone, or something, now has the power to interfere with stetting. Imagine it. We're a federation of worlds, light-years apart; we just can't hang together without stet . . . the result would be utter chaos!'

Abruptly, his shoulders went back. 'We've got to move now, Neale. Alert our forces for police action.'

8

Technical switch

Keston returned slowly to consciousness. His head felt muzzy and his limbs, like leaden weights, no longer part of him. He lay on a hard couch, above him a high white ceiling. Plain walls and a door. The faint hum of an air-conditioning unit hummed somewhere behind him, and he turned his head.

A wall-sized stereo panel came into focus, bringing him a view of a city; a rigidly planned city, antiseptic and cold, square miles of metal and concrete and glass and plastic, spanned by functional bridges and served by robo-vehicles. He stared, struggling to comprehend.

The shadow of a man fell upon the screen and Keston, head hammering, sat upright on the couch. The room was larger than he'd first supposed, but just as austere; the man, tall and thin-faced with intense dark eyes, wore a plain white robe and held out a goblet. They were alone in the room.

'Drink this and you'll feel better.'

Keston sipped cautiously. His memory prickled, and he asked:

'Copper?'

The tall man spoke quietly. 'If you are referring to your D'Amazone guard, she is unharmed. She caused some damage before the gas overcame her — we took the precaution of disarming and locking her in a cell.'

Copper wouldn't like that, Keston thought, and shook his head to clear away the last of his mental cobwebs. He remembered Honeymoon . . . the receiving booth had been filled with knock-out gas. He looked again at the wall screen, at white-overalled men busy with intricate machinery; they swarmed like ants, single-minded, obsessed by their work.

Realization dawned on him. 'This isn't Neoism,' he blurted out.

'That is correct.' The gaunt man appeared to be amused. 'Allow me to introduce myself. I am Redmont, of

Technos.' He bowed stiffly.

Technos! Impossible, Keston thought wildly, and then: *How*? Fear mounted in him, and he shivered. 'It was you who tried to kill me on Park, and again on the Junkworld!'

Redmont shook his head. 'No, that would be Deterling, I suspect. On the contrary, I have a use for you, alive, which is why I had you brought here.'

'Brought here?'

The Autarch smiled thinly. 'Of course. Did you think your arrival here was an accident? We are the most highly developed technically of all the Federation worlds — you should know that if you've given any thought to the situation at all. Our technicians have perfected a device for controlling stetting operations from a distance. They call it the stet-switch.'

Keston stared at him incredulously. 'You mean you can interfere with stetting? Snatch people?'

'Crudely put . . . technically, your space-time-energy co-ordinates were altered by remote control when you entered the booth on Honeymoon. Our superior control enabled us to redirect you here.'

Keston staggered under the idea. Could anyone really do that? But he couldn't doubt he was on Technos . . . it meant nobody who stetted was safe. It meant breakdown in galactic travel. It meant the end of the Federation.

Fear came crawling back. 'If you don't mean us harm, bring Copper to me.'

'Later,' Redmont said, 'when you have agreed to do what I want.'

'And that is?'

'Barnabas set you to script a biography of the Edens. He even arranged a meeting for you with Kyle Eden. True?'

Keston could only nod.

'Good. It is not easy to reach Eden, and I want to, so — you shall be my ambassador. You will carry a message to him, a proposition from me, and do your utmost to persuade him to accept.'

Keston felt bewildered, wondering what was coming next.

'In return, I shall open our Intelligence files to you. We have acquired considerable information about the Edens. I'm sure you will be interested.'

Keston thought fast. It sounded like a good deal, if Redmont could be trusted. 'Agreed,' he said quickly.

'I thought you would agree, Mr. Keston.' The Autarch sat down carefully in a stiff-backed chair. 'Let me explain . . . Technos is expanding, as you will have heard already. But not why this is necessary. Unlike Mogul, it is not simple conquest we are interested in, but progress . . .

'Yes, progress is our dream. Only technology can enable man to progress, and we have that technology. We have the most advanced social system in the Federation, but we are not too selfish to share our good fortune.'

His words rolled smoothly off the tongue, with practiced ease, but his eyes glittered. A fanatic, Keston thought warily.

Redmont went on: 'Yet there are some so misguided that they would misunderstand our motives, some who would resist good fortune. Our system must be imposed for their own good, by force if necessary . . . we alone can prevent

Deterling building himself an empire.'

Deterling — Redmont, Keston thought; what's the difference? But he carefully kept his thought to himself.

The Autarch smiled benignly. 'As you will imagine, there could be some opposition to our plans. But suppose — ' He leaned forward in his chair, eager. 'Suppose Eden were to come forward and take the lead? Suppose the father-figure of legend decided to help the poorer worlds? I think most people would accept him. Eden then, as a figure-head, backed by our technology . . . '

Keston sat stunned, his natural skepticism vanquished. For a moment, he looked at Redmont with something like admiration. The plan had a touch of genius. The legendary hero of pop mythology backed by weapons of a superior technology — it couldn't fail. Not with the stet-switch thrown in. United Worlds would be swept away, relegated to the dusty shelves of history. The Federation would come under the control of one world, Technos, and one man, Redmont. The idea sent a chill through him.

Eden might have other ideas, of course
. . . in fact, Eden should be told about
this right away. And UW.

'I'll deliver your message,' he said,
forcing a lightness he did not feel into his
voice. 'Now let me see your files — and I
want my guard back. I'll feel happier with
her around.'

Redmont pressed a button on his chair.
'Bring in the D'Amazone,' he said to
somebody outside the room. They waited
in silence.

The door slid open. From the passage
outside came the sounds of a struggle.
Keston saw Adrienne, her arms bound,
dragged into the room between four
armed and badly flustered men. One of
them had blood on his face; another
appeared winded. They all looked as if
they'd tangled with a wildcat.

'Men!' Adrienne spat out, breasts
heaving. 'Take your filthy hands off me!'
Her tawny eyes blazed in anger and she
jerked about like a trapped animal.

Keston smiled. 'Relax, Copper,' he
drawled. 'Everything's all right now.'

She darted a look at him, and her

stocky body stilled. Silent, she looked round the room, staring long at Redmont. Slowly, she relaxed.

'Turn her loose,' Keston ordered. 'And give her back her gun.'

One of the guards protested: 'Reverend Autarch, this woman is dangerous!'

Redmont looked thoughtfully at her. 'Mr. Keston, there must be no trouble, you understand? I hold you responsible for her good behaviour.'

Keston, repressing a smile, nodded. It amused him to have their roles reversed . . . but Redmont did well to beware the wrath of a guard of D'Amazone. She had been humiliated, separated from her client, male hands laid on her. Copper would feel that her honour had been tarnished, and was not likely to forgive the outrage.

'Behave yourself, Copper,' he said, 'You can see I'm unharmed — and I've made a deal with these people.'

The Autarch said: 'Certainly, neither of you is in any danger. You are my guests.' He gestured, and a guard cut her bonds. Another reluctantly handed back her laser gun.

Adrienne grabbed the gun, tense, holding it as if contemplating taking immediate revenge. She glared sullenly at her captors ... her treatment was something she wouldn't forget in a hurry. But she holstered the gun ...

Keston began breathing again. He turned to Redmont. 'Now,' he said, 'your files on the Eden Clan, please.'

* * *

Venner was a long way from home. A small man, neat in dress and habit, he felt uncomfortable in rough peasant's cloak with several days' stubble on his chin; unhappy about his alliance with one of Mogul's more arrogant nobles — and definitely uneasy in his role of spy. He knew he would die unpleasantly if anyone suspected that he came from Technos.

He checked the thought abruptly, slamming down his tankard of ale on the tavern table. 'A thousand curses on this poxy power rationing,' he growled.

The black-uniformed noble sprawled in

a carved chair opposite smiled contemptuously. 'Quite unnecessary,' he agreed. 'Sun power is efficient enough. The batteries provide more than we need — but Deterling must hoard power for his armies. War and conquest are all he dreams of.'

Venner nodded, looking out through the tavern window. Sunset shadows almost obliterated the grim outline of the fortress on top of the hill above the town.

He withdrew his gaze through the curtains of their private room and spoke with rough confidence. Above all, he must give this would-be assassin confidence — the last rays of sunlight caught the bare skulls posted on poles outside the castle gates.

'It will be easy enough. I have one of the new type laser guns — an improved model.'

As Venner laid the shining weapon on the table, Lord Gould straightened in his chair. For a moment, cunning overlaid the arrogance of his features. 'Where did you get this?'

Venner shrugged, wondering whether

or not to drop a hint that Eden was involved. He knew the men of Mogul believed the legend. He contented himself with, 'Off-world,' and repeated: 'It will be easy enough. You alone are ready to take the reins of power. With Deterling dead, you can move into the fortress — no one can touch you there.'

The Lord Gould echoed his words. 'Aye, easy enough — with Deterling dead.'

Venner suppressed a feeling of contempt. These barbaric nobles were all the same; always plotting revolt, but never making a move. The feudal system sapped a man's will, he decided, and looked into the shadows gathering in a corner of the room to hide his expression. Think as a man of Mogul would, he reminded himself . . .

Gould mumbled, 'Aye, the people will follow my lead once I've gained power. Nothing is more certain. 'Tis only removing Deterling that is uncertain.'

Venner took the gun in his hands. Skillfully, he worked the mechanism — it was uncharged — testing the sights and firing stud. 'You load it here . . . it has a range up to a quarter of a mile. So you don't even have to get near him, just take a clear sighting and — '

Gould watched his practiced hands, fascinated. Then — 'How much?' he asked.

'One thousand credits.'

'Aye, I'll take it — but not a word mind — and pay you after I've gained the fortress.'

Venner's voice went flat. 'No sire, you pay me one half now, one half later.'

'A quarter now . . . '

Venner appeared to hesitate. Above all, he must not seem too anxious to make a sale. As if the words were being dragged out of him, he said: 'Very well, a quarter now.' And added quickly, 'but I shall claim the balance the moment I hear you have succeeded.'

Gould lowered his eyes, staring at the plastic tabletop. 'Aye, do that.'

Do that, and die, Venner thought grimly, and conjured avarice into his face as the noble drew out a small pouch. He waited, with mock impatience, while

Gould undid the clasp and counted out coins.

Rising, he swept the coins into his hand, put them away under his cloak. He picked up the gun and inserted the charge. 'You're in business now — good luck, sire.'

Venner went out through the door in hurried strides and down the stairs to the street. He waited in the shadow of an arch until he saw Gould hasten away, and then moved to a public call box and dialled the fortress.

He hummed a marching refrain popular on Mogul as he waited for the connection to be made, insisted on speaking to security — and somebody high up at that — keeping his own screen blank.

He said: 'Lord Gould and other nobles are plotting to kill the ruler. They have obtained a long-range gun from off-world. Immediately after the assassination, they plan a coup to seize the whole planet. *You must act at once!*'

Before the Security man could ask questions, Venner broke the connection and ran for the nearest stet station; he did not want to be on Mogul when the trouble started. He chuckled as he ran . . . for the moment Deterling would be too busy holding down a rebellion to bother invading other worlds.

9

The Eden Dossier

'Our technology, the most advanced in the galaxy, is based on fusion power, Mr. Keston,' Quinn said.

Keston grunted monosyllabically. He was growing tired of hearing how advanced Technos was, and how they had to expand for the good of others.

Quinn, Redmont's chief of Intelligence, had an egg-shaped head, a baby's face and puckered lips. His voice was coldly polite. 'We use fusion power for everything, heating, lighting, transport, industry. We find it most efficient.'

The big car toured silently along a wide apparently deserted throughway between austere buildings. Looking out, Keston could hardly tell offices from apartment blocks or industrial plant; they were all depressingly alike. He sat in the back of the car, between Quinn and Adrienne, aware of her disapproval for his making this deal, but still feeling safer because she was there. She had hardly spoken a word to him since leaving Redmont . . . a D'Amazone had been insulted and she resembled a quart of fury in a pint pot.

He glimpsed a group of white-overalled technicians at work on some unrecognizable machine; they had the immense concentration of ants in an anthill, and he was glad he didn't have to live permanently on Technos. The place was too much like a beehive, antiseptic, lacking all human feeling.

They passed one impressive building that soared to the sky; fluted columns supported arches that ended in a magnificent spire. A stream of people passed reverently in and out through massive ornate doors.

'A cathedral?' Keston hazarded.

'No . . . that is our main power station,' Quinn answered proudly. 'Inspiring, isn't it? One day, perhaps, Mr. Keston, you will script the history of Technos . . . '

'Perhaps,' Keston said, a shade more grimly than he intended. But it added up.

Technology was a religion on this world.

The car moved on, swiftly, silently, to stop outside a windowless cube of concrete. They got out and, at the door, Quinn showed a pass.

'This way, please.'

The Intelligence chief's manner changed now. He hurried Keston and his guard along a plain corridor, as if afraid the blank walls might reveal secrets, to a lift gate; they dropped to a subterranean area, a vast cavern with walls of glowing light and the steady hum of air-conditioning plant.

Keston noted with amazement that most of the area had been hastily screened off. Quinn turned at right angles to the screens and walked rapidly down a bare side corridor, opening the first door he came to. The room was small, with one table and chair, a viewer and recording discs, a grey metal filing cabinet.

Quinn locked the door.

Keston's curiosity was back; he could smell a story coming and suppressed his instinctive desire to flee this world. Apparently Redmont intended to keep his side of the bargain. 'I want everything you have on Eden,' he said crisply. 'Everything.'

Quinn nodded, adjusting the viewer and inserting a disc. He dimmed the wall lights and a screen glowed to life . . .

The first shots showed Eden's world, from far out in space — taken through a telescope, Keston decided. Eden didn't allow unofficial visitors near his home world.

The planet was bigger than Keston had anticipated, swinging through the dark void against a background of stars. The dull glow of volcanoes lit its surface. Eden's World circled no sun; an eternal wanderer, it travelled across the galaxy — and Keston wondered where it had started its inconceivable journey, and where it would end. He remembered the Fool's third riddle as he looked . . .

No Earth-type world this. Warmed only by its internal radioactive fires, here Eden was reported to live alone, served by robots. Alone except for his Beast.

Quinn said: 'He always maintains contact with whichever world is nearest to him, of course. His local power is absolute.'

And that was why Redmont needed *him*, Keston thought. No one went there, except by invitation.

Quinn inserted another disc into the viewer. 'Historical,' he said briefly.

This one showed a world Keston did not immediately recognize. A world of anarchy, lawless, with every man in competition with his neighbour; a society in which only the ruthless survived. There was a sequence with Eden riding his Beast through the streets.

'Morg Eden . . .'

The picture was not sharply focused and Keston strained to see his features. He could not tell Morg from Alain; they had the same build, the same stance and gestures. And now he remembered the planet. Morg, as hero; it had been a police state before he came and — in pop legend Eden had led the people to freedom.

In this case, freedom equalled anarchy.

Quinn murmured: 'Morg Eden made millions here, dealing in all the things

— those little luxuries you take for granted and don't miss until they're taken away — banned by the previous regime. Of course, a few hundred thousand were killed in the process . . . but those who survived thought Eden a god.'

A picture of a young woman flashed on the screen and disappeared.

'Morg's wife . . . she died in mysterious circumstances soon after David Eden was born. I have a theory,' the Intelligence chief said, 'that the Edens murder their wives immediately following the firstborn. At least, it's strange that we've never been able to trace a medical record for any of the Eden Clan.'

Adrienne muttered, 'Just like men!' and Keston looked warningly at her. She glared back.

The next film started with two planets circling a sun and, as the camera moved in, Keston knew what was coming. Neither world had any large land mass; on one, artificial cities floated — on the other, the colonists had taken to the air, living in drifting sky-trailers. There had been no need for war between them . . .

116

For the first time, watching this secret film, Keston understood how it had started. David Eden, representing an armaments world, began by selling one planet a few second-hand weapons. Then he set war rumors circulating on the other planet. Bribing and blackmailing, telling any lie that came to mind, he manipulated them, playing one against the other — building up his own private war and selling weapons to both sides. And demanding a larger cut of the profits from the manufacturers.

Keston, sick, watched interplanetary war flare up, and remembered how close they were to galactic war.

'United Worlds finally exposed him,' Quinn said, 'and he bolted — with a few more millions for the clan treasury. The Edens were the richest family in the galaxy by now, the most powerful, the only family with their own planet. David grew cautious . . .'

Quinn switched off the viewer and lit the walls behind. He opened the metal filing cabinet and brought out plasti-metal sheets.

'From the documentary evidence here, you will see that no Eden operated for long on any one world. They kept shifting the focus of their attention. The whole clan seem governed by an obsession. Again and again, one or the other acted as a rep for new inventions, helping to spread them throughout the Federation — to their own increasing profit. The ultimate percentage men.

'Now here — ' Quinn turned over more sheets as Keston studied them. 'Here, you will begin to understand the true nature of the legend that has grown up around them.'

Keston's brain whirled as he read how the Edens, under a false name, had started the Eden Clan supporters club, with a branch on every colonized world. And more; there was evidence to show that the record had been deliberately faked, historical documents destroyed and forgeries inserted to cover up gaps in the past.

With every sheet he turned, one fact stood out: the legend was fiction, designed by the Edens.

Quinn smiled as he closed the file. 'David's wife, too, died soon after Kyle was born.'

Keston looked at Adrienne, and took a deep breath. 'It's time for a showdown with Kyle Eden, Copper — let's go!'

⋆ ⋆ ⋆

Deterling relaxed on a silken couch, one hand clutching a wine cup, the other the black-haired Magda. It was pleasant to relax with a woman, his plans for the invasion of Freedom complete, his armies ready to move at a moment's notice. He waited, now, only for news from Terra.

Freedom was a weak world. Originally colonized by a minor political party, their descendants called it the 'People's Planet' — government was by an unwieldy council on which every minority group had to be represented. There was only a titular head of state.

Decisions were made by majority vote of the whole council in session; a time-consuming method. Deterling had no doubt at all that he would control the

119

planet before Freedom's council even had time to meet.

He smiled at the thought, and pulled Magda closer. 'You're a satisfying woman,' he murmured.

Time passed pleasantly enough until the wall drapes parted with a *swish* and his Security chief hurried in. 'Your pardon, sire! Assassination and rebellion are plotted. Lord Gould — '

Deterling rose, brushing Magda away, buttoning his uniform. 'Gould, is it? We'll see about that one . . . tell me the details.'

'The fortress is secure, sire, your guards alerted. The warning came from an anonymous caller — unfortunately, the call box was empty when my men arrived. According to the caller, Gould has the backing of other nobles — and a new-type weapon.'

'So!' Deterling chuckled, rubbing his hands. 'A new weapon.' Revolt had always been an occupational hazard for the rulers of Mogul, and he was prepared. 'We'll let Gould have his head, for the moment.' He jerked on a bell-rope, and waited.

Presently, a broad man with a bald head, dressed in black, came into the room. Deterling walked round him, inspecting him closely, nodding satisfaction; the man was near enough his double to fool anyone at a distance. 'The battlements,' he ordered.

Deterling climbed a flight of stone steps behind his double, paused at a door leading onto a fortress tower. 'All right, show yourself,' he growled.

The double walked forward and leaned on the stone wall, staring out over a patchwork of fields and the road leading to the town at the bottom of the hill. Moonlight revealed drifting cloud. Yellow windows winked at him. 'I can see armed men gathering in the streets,' he called back.

Behind him, sheltering under a massive stone arch, Deterling looked grim. So it was not another false alarm. 'Let them come. I'll show these lords who rules Mogul!'

They waited, Deterling congratulating himself on his cunning, his double bathed in moonlight . . .

Suddenly, a bright flash showed in the distance, lighting the night like day, and a beam of concentrated light struck the double. He recoiled, burning like a meteor, and died within seconds.

'That laser,' Deterling said to his security chief. 'It's good — get it for me!' He moved cautiously, keeping in shadow, to the edge of the tower, watching armed men swarm up the hill from the town. 'Rabble,' he jeered. 'We'll teach them a lesson — now!'

He snapped an order and it was relayed. The gates of the fortress creaked open and Deterling's personal guard poured out.

The dictator dressed in protective armor and followed behind at a safe distance, shouting: 'Bring me Gould — I want his head — a handsome reward to the men who bring me Lord Gould!'

The rival armies clashed on the hill-slope. Weapons crackled — and then they set to at close quarters. Knives flashed and metal crunched on bone. For a time there was no decision.

Then the rebels — seeing Deterling still

alive — wavered and fell back. Deterling's black-clad guard, bearing downhill, had an advantage, and chased the rebels into the town. The screams of the wounded rose to the moon and blood seeped along the gutters as the slaughter intensified.

Flares lit the night sky and shots echoed between the buildings. Pressed into dark corners the rebels fought for their lives. Swords bit into flesh and lasers burned.

'Spare none of them,' Deterling shouted wildly. 'Kill all the traitors!'

A fire started, but nobody bothered with it. Bodies piled up as house-to-house fighting reached a new savagery. Men were dragged into the street and butchered like cattle as the flames rose higher.

Two guards dragged Lord Gould before Deterling. The Security chief held out the assassination weapon.

Deterling tried it out on a group of prisoners, grunted satisfaction. 'Good, good, we must have more of these to use against Freedom.' He stared grimly at the captured noble. 'Where did you get it, traitor? Speak up!'

'Off-world,' Gould mumbled. 'Your mercy, sire . . . '

'Mercy?' Deterling spat. 'Bring me a sword — and a pole for this cur's head.'

Anger blazed in him. Revolt now — when he needed every man with him for the invasion. It meant delay while he regrouped, made sure of the other nobles' loyalty.

He took the sword offered him and swung it to test the balance. Gould was forced to his knees, babbling. Deterling lifted the sword high for the death stroke.

* * *

Neale was uneasy. A frown creased his young-looking face under wavy gray hair. He had given the necessary orders to set a United Worlds police action in motion — but he could not see the end of it. Some time must pass before any results, effective or otherwise could be known. And time was against him.

Wainwright's deputy left UW headquarters in a worried frame of mind. Flowers' report still disturbed him; how could Keston have vanished like that? Was it really possible for anyone to interfere with a stetting operation? Just thinking about it gave him a headache.

Neale — he had long since discarded his given names — had plans of his own. United Worlds was all-important to Terra's economy, and that made the post of Director-General a plum — and he was close to snatching the prize.

One day, not too far off, he would be Neale of Terra. His name, he recalled, meant champion, chieftain. But he wasn't running alone, and now it was time to insist on some co-operation.

He signalled his private car from the pool and settled comfortably in the back. His chauffeur headed out into Terra's overcrowded traffic lanes, crawling between skyscraper blocks; so Neale had ample time to study the vehicles behind and make sure he was not followed.

'Norma's place,' he said quietly.

The chauffeur waited a chance to swing off the main boulevard and threaded a path through a maze of slow moving traffic. Neale relaxed, confident that no one suspected this discreet apartment he kept was for a purpose other than meeting his current mistress. No doubt security knew of it — and turned a blind eye. The thought made him smile.

He dismissed his chauffeur, watched the car move away, and let himself into the apartment. It was furnished in quiet taste, with nothing to arouse suspicion.

'Norma?' he called softly.

He had ensured she would be out; but he was a careful man and checked everything.

He moved into the bedroom, smelling her perfume, and opened a sliding wall panel; stepped through into the next-door apartment he rented under another name. This was sparsely furnished, dusty. He picked up a communicator set with a blanked-off screen, and left by a different door.

At the street corner he descended to the rolling road-strip and traveled to a distant stet-station. Neon-ads flashed past.

HEXY IS SEXY . . . LEARN WITH SLEEPEZY

When he arrived, he told the operator, 'Mogul' but he hesitated before entering a booth. Remembering Keston, fear gripped him. Suppose he, too, somehow disappeared? Neale fought down panic. To get anywhere you've got to take some risk, he argued with himself.

The moment of waiting passed, and he stepped out on Mogul. His relief was temporary. The sound of fighting echoed from the street. Running to the doorway he looked out into the night, saw sprawling bodies lit by the glare of fires. A quick look told him who was fighting; the armies of rival nobles.

So Deterling had a rebellion on his hands.

Neale scowled, cursing Mogul's feudal system. The timing, so far as he was concerned, was all wrong. Premature. Well, there was no point in using the communicator now. He'd have to work this out alone.

He backed into the stet station, always considered a neutral zone. 'Terra,' he said briefly.

As he waited in the booth, the seconds

seemed to last for ever. But now he had further worry. His mind raced. What was he going to do?

Wainwright was past it, in both senses. Neale laughed harshly, showing his teeth, white and even. His diversion seemed to be working out, and he didn't care whether Deterling fell or not . . . but now he would have to go the rest of the way on his own.

It was time to act, time to take over.

He arrived back on Terra, left the booth and took the roadway to his hidden apartment, making sure that he entered unobserved. He exchanged the communicator for a miniature needle-gun, loading it carefully.

He slipped the gun into his pocket and considered his next move. He'd need an alibi. He went next door and put through a call to Norma.

Then he went out on the street, his face glistening with sweat, his expression intense as he listened to the phrase that pulsed through his head, over and over again . . . *Neale of Terra*!

10

Change of Director

Keston's first glimpse of Neoism was an immense vista of olive-green vigorously slashed across orange. It was several moments before he realized he was staring at a wall-sized painting in the abstract manner, facing the stet booth. Poised in front of it, and gently turning in the breeze, stood a gold mobile; he watched it, fascinated, but unable to decide what it represented.

This was a planet colonized by artists, the trendsetter in galactic art.

Adrienne looked blankly at the abstract and said sourly: 'Where now, ambassador?'

Keston turned on her, half-angry. 'Lay off that ambassador stuff — I got us off Technos, didn't I?'

He looked quickly behind him, expecting Quinn's spies to be following. There was no one. So maybe Redmont took the ambassador bit seriously . . .

Adrienne muttered, 'Redmont! I'll — '

'Forget him,' Keston said.

In the fresh air of Neoism, Redmont's plan to make use of the Eden legend did not seem so dangerous. After all, what could one man, one world even, really do against the combined might of the Federation? United Worlds would stop him soon enough, Keston felt confident.

They walked across a public square to the travellers' hotel, passing groups of casually-dressed Neoists engaged in animated discussion; and others, lost to this world judging by their dreamy expressions.

A fragment of conversation drifted after them: 'Organic paint is dead, I tell you — bio-sculpt is the latest thing . . . '

In the hotel lobby, a desk clerk was working on a complicated floor mosaic. He glanced up and called cheerfully, 'Shan't be a minute!'

Several minutes passed, and Keston began to fret with impatience. Time did not seem to be important here. At last, the clerk cemented the final piece of a floor section in place and went behind his desk, pushing a ledger towards them.

'Clerking's only a part-time job,' he explained. 'Here, everything is a part-time job, except art. Everyone does their stint of public service, just to keep things running, though you may find you'll have to wait a while.'

Keston signed in and booked a double room. They followed the clerk's directions — he had gone back to his mosaic — and Adrienne opened a door and stood staring into their room.

Over her shoulder, Keston saw walls of violently different colours, some with diagonal stripes, some patterned with random dots. The ceiling was a uniform blood-red. The furniture, of a sickly yellow hue, seemed to have been designed by non-humans — for non-humans.

'The latest style, I suppose,' Keston said warily.

Adrienne sneered. 'Degenerate!'

They showered, and ate in the dining room. By ignoring the decor, Keston found he was able to enjoy his meal;

131

cooking was treated as an art on Neoism. Even his D'Amazone appeared to relish a change from her normal Spartan diet.

Afterwards, Keston returned to the desk where — after another, longer wait — he composed and sent a stet message with his latest tape to Barnabas. Then he enquired about transport to Eden's world.

'There are no rockets here, only solar wind craft,' the clerk explained cheerfully. 'We like to take life easy. Anyway, sailing's an art too, you know.'

Keston nodded, thoughtful. He had done a bit of space-sailing, for sport; it looked as though he'd be getting more practice. 'Can I get in touch with Eden from here?'

'Of course — ' Keston remembered how Eden exerted local power — 'By laser beam, direct.'

He composed a message, apologizing for his delay in arrival, and it was beamed across space. An answer flashed back within minutes:

Welcome! I am looking forward to your early arrival. Kyle Eden.

'Space port'll be shut down for the night,' the clerk said. 'Leave it till morning, huh?' He got on with his mosaic.

Keston went back to his room while Adrienne muttered, 'Eden . . . that fiction factory!' Again she checked the room for security, and Keston began to undress for bed. An authoritative rap sounded on the door.

Adrienne's gun seamed to jump into her hand as she waved him back. Keston's heart fluttered as the door opened. It was Flowers, the UW agent who stood there, looking disgusted.

He came striding in, demanding: 'What the hell happened to you, Keston? I've been waiting around on this half-baked planet on the off chance you'd show up. I only just found out you were here — these damned Neoists have no idea of time!'

Keston stared at him, wondering. 'You certainly get around . . . ' But Flowers didn't take the hint, so he sighed and filled him in on Redmont's stet-switch and the plan to use Eden in a takeover bid.

Flowers groaned and swore. 'Stet-switch is bad enough — but you haven't heard the rest. Wainwright's been assassinated . . . United Worlds is in an uproar!'

★ ★ ★

Neale smiled as he stood alone on the great dais, facing the assembly of United Worlds council members, waiting for the noise to die down. There were more of them present than he'd expected at such short notice; more than fifty of them, filling the front rows of seats in the conference hall at UW headquarters. Delegates from a bizarre variety of communities. He recognized the Sheikh of Necca, a silent unmoving figure, hawk-nosed and brown-skinned under a flowing burnous; a stout, angry-looking farmer from Botan; and an angular prim-faced woman from Psycho — he'd always disapproved of Psycho's joining the Federation; it was quite impossible for an off-worlder to tell the doctors from the patients, so closely had they interbred.

As the noise began to die away, Neale,

dressed in a formal grey suit with a flower in his buttonhole, raised a hand and spoke quietly into the microphone.

'Wainwright has gone. This is a great personal loss for me, and a severe blow to United Worlds . . . '

Like hell it is, he thought; *it was a pleasure to get rid of the bastard.*

'His murderer — a maniac, and not responsible for his action, I feel sure — is being vigorously sought by Terran police. He will quickly be caught and turned over to Psycho for treatment.'

Some chance of that!

'Meanwhile, as acting Director-General until the new election is held, I ask for your support at this difficult time. I have temporarily stopped the UW police action — it seemed to me this was an infringement of the non-interference pact, and that a decision to pursue this policy should only be taken by a majority vote of the full council.'

The farmer from Botan, red-faced, broke in heatedly: 'What about Technos? Redmont still boasts of his plan to expand — and we're nearest to him. Botan is an agricultural world. We just don't have the weapon-power to fight him. We demand UW action now!'

'And Mogul,' the delegate from Freedom shouted. 'Deterling must be stopped too!'

'Let them fight it out between themselves,' suggested the member for a planet far removed from either Technos or Mogul. 'UW should certainly not interfere in the internal government of any member world of the Federation. That would be an infringement of the charter.'

'Give Eden a chance — '

The uproar started again, one member shouting down another, and Neale said, smiling: 'One at a time, please. You will all get the chance to put your point of view. Right now, the member for Pedestar has the floor.'

He sat down on the dais-throne, a dignified figure, his face composed to indicate concentration. He was bored, but dare not show it. The speeches went on, and on, the talk drifted, and he was content to allow it to drift. Above all, he must avoid any challenge to the chair.

This was power, he thought, and felt content. But first, he must consolidate his position; changes could come later. He encouraged the clash of interests, playing one world against another; with the council divided, no action could be taken.

He sat quietly, looking out over the chamber, at the heads of world-states, thoughtful. For the moment, he was satisfied to be accepted as acting Director-General; he studied faces, picking out those most likely to support him at election time. As Deputy, he had the best chance anyway.

His fingers began to drum idly. Should he throw in a hint about Keston's disappearance while stetting? He still felt uneasy about it himself, and decided not. He would keep that up his sleeve to cover any later emergency.

He sat dreaming . . . with this takeover he was, in effect, Neale of Terra.

11

No wandering light

' . . . Four . . . three . . . two . . . one
. . . *blast off*!'

Keston sweated and itched under the
safety straps securing him in his deep
foam-lined cradle as he lay listening to
the pilot's countdown. Across the cabin
from him, Adrienne lay relaxed, calm as a
D'Amazone before battle.

The fiery roar of the rockets deafened
him; the walls of the small spaceship
vibrated urgently. He was unhappily
aware that he rested in close proximity to
several tons of highly explosive fuel and
that accidents could — and did — happen to these outdated chemical rocket
ships.

Through the thick glassite porthole he
had a distorted view of the spaceport
— buildings and launch pad — moving
away from him. Then acceleration shoved

him deep down into his cradle.

Flowers was back there on Neoism, worrying over Wainwright's death and what would happen to UW . . .

Seconds built into minutes, and the ferry's motor cut off its thrust and coasted towards the orbital rendezvous. Keston's muscles slackened.

The pilot's drawling voice cane over the intercom: 'Nothing to do now but wait. In a few minutes, you'll see the yachts.'

Beyond the porthole, Neoism, a drab green-and-brown ball, receded. The sky above the atmosphere took on a deep blue-black shade; a few stars shone with startling clearness.

Then, as the ship slanted into orbit, Keston saw the gigantic sails of the solar wind craft, filling the sky with silver triangles. There were, perhaps, a dozen of them orbiting Neoism, each with its tiny capsule slung below.

The ferry pilot fired his retro-rocket briefly, matching speed and direction with one of the space-sailors; the two ships drifted closer and magnets clamped their hulls together.

As Keston and Adrienne un-strapped, the pilot said: '*Firefly*'s all checked out and ready to sail. You sure you know how to handle her?'

'I'll remember the drill . . . '

'Good luck, then.'

Keston and Adrienne moved through the double-lock, into the sailer's capsule. The ferry pilot fired his booster, and the two ships left orbit and headed into open space; then he demagnetized and used his retro and dropped back towards Neoism.

Watching the brief flare of rocket fire, Keston felt strictly on his own. He studied a star chart display, checked their position and programmed the computer to set a course.

'It's at a time like this, Copper,' he said, 'that you learn to appreciate stetting — this trip will take days.'

Adrienne shrugged. 'At least we'll get there.'

Yes, Keston thought, no danger of Redmont snatching them again, or a bullet from an assassin. He was safe now, on the last leg of his mission — providing he didn't make a hash of sailing the *Firefly*.

Keston reviewed procedure in his mind, checking equipment. The space-sailer relied on light pressure from the sun for power. He began trimming the gigantic sail — metal foil, thin as the wall of a soap bubble — by winching the spider's-web rigging. Slowly, almost imperceptibly, they moved away from Neoism's sun.

Firefly's speed built up gradually from the impetus given by the ferry rocket, but it built up continuously. Fuel cost nothing — that was the big advantage of solar wind craft. Light radiation striking the sail gave constant acceleration; the longer the trip, the faster they moved.

And *Firefly* handled well; light as a feather blown before a gale, she sailed out into the void, building speed. An hour passed and Neoism began to shift position; space was dead black, the stars bright and unwinking

Tension left Keston. He whistled gaily as he made a navigation check and used the winch to adjust the trim of the sail. 'Haven't done this for years,' he said conversationally. 'Riding a sunbeam, we used to call it.'

Adrienne sat on a bunk, smiling. 'You're like a child with a new toy.'

Keston laughed. 'Maybe!' He'd have to take up the sport again; hadn't felt so carefree in years.

Firefly sailed the great ocean of space, clipping along, a tiny capsule under a vast silver sail, heading out for Eden's World . . .

The capsule was very small, and cramped for two people. And the trip was going to be long and slow. Keston sat on the bunk opposite Adrienne, looking at her, and it occurred to him that for the next few days he was going to be alone with a woman.

A guard of D'Amazone — a woman? Well . . . of course, she was — and virgin at that, he supposed. He became aware, for the first time of the feminine contours of her body and sexual pressure grew inside him. It took an effort to remind himself that she belonged to a society that had no use for men.

The situation was intriguing — and

frustrating. He laughed again, but harshly now.

'What is it, Keston?' Then she seemed to read his mind and rose. 'I'll see about a meal for us.'

They ate and slept, Keston restless. Waking, he checked their position and adjusted the sail to a new angle of the sun. Speed was increasing satisfactorily, but there wasn't a lot to do. *Firefly* sailed herself.

His thoughts dwelt more and more on Copper, and that was not so satisfactory. In the confines of their tiny capsule, he could not easily avoid looking at her, and each time he looked, she appeared lovelier, more desirable. Her bare legs under the short tunic began to attract like magnets. Tawny eyes watched him with . . . interest?

He sweated, and then it occurred to him . . . 'This the first time you've been shut up with a man like this?'

Adrienne said: 'I can look after myself.'

And of course, she could. Keston faced the fact that he was no match for a fighting D'Amazone.

143

But as the trip lasted — and he made himself busy with minute adjustments to the sail — his romantic feeling for her grew. Love? He shook himself — a guard of D'Amazone did not admit the emotion existed.

He was glad when Eden's World registered on the radar. Now he had real work to do; calculate an orbit and sail *Firefly* to the artificial satellite circling the planet.

Eden's World was incredibly hard to see, a mere pinpoint in the void. He remembered the Fool's third riddle . . . '*Dark as night . . . no wandering light.*' With no sun of its own, only starlight showed the dark globe from a distance.

He felt excited as *Firefly* glided into orbit. He was going to meet Kyle Eden, the last of the legendary clan. Adrienne seemed unaffected by the idea.

Keston docked the sailer at his first attempt; something to be proud of. He tuned in the radio and a voice (Eden's?) said: 'There is a rocket coming up for you.'

They waited, staring at the dull rim of the planet turning below, its surface red with the reflected glare of volcanoes. The rocket arrived and they transferred and strapped themselves down. The pilot-less rocket plummeted down towards the sunless wanderer and Keston wondered exactly what waited for him below. Eden's home. Soon he would be face to face with the mythical hero . . .

The silver sail of the yacht shrank above them. The rocket landed automatically on its retros. The landing pad sank smoothly below the surface of the planet, down, down, coming to rest in a huge cavern. A panel slid open.

Adrienne un-strapped first and moved to the opening, looking out, hand on gun-butt. Keston followed her and, over her shoulder, stared into the familiar face of Kyle Eden.

'Welcome, Keston,' Eden said. 'I hear Barnabas is making a big production of my stereo biography . . . well, I can give you plenty of new material for the script.' He seemed genuinely pleased to see Keston, pointedly ignored his

145

D'Amazone guard. 'How are my Supporters' clubs doing? Well, I hope?'

Keston nodded, puzzled by his reception. This wasn't quite what he had expected.

Eden's face showed pride. 'Yes, the legend's done well . . . and we'll improve on it yet. Put our heads together and think up something special. I've got lots of stories that haven't been used before.'

Keston stared blankly, wondering if he were dreaming. He recalled Copper's phrase, 'A fiction factory!' And suddenly it dawned on him why he had been allowed this visit; Eden took his legend seriously and was still concerned with adding to it.

He took a long breath. Go easy, he warned himself, let him tell it his way. Now was not the moment to insist that all he wanted was the truth behind the legend. He glanced sideways at Adrienne and saw her lip curl back in scorn.

Eden whistled, and his Beast came trotting out of the shadows. It was clearly an animal, Keston saw, but not quite like any other; ponderous and dapple-grey, its single straight horn gleamed in the reflected light. There was an ornate saddle strapped to its back and Eden swung up.

Something about the way Eden looked and moved, bothered Keston. The handsome rugged face of a thousand stereo tapes was instantly recognizable, of course, but the features appeared overlain with — with what? A pattern of minute lines, like a very old oil painting that had begun to crack. And the way he held his body, stiffly, as though it were fragile . . .

'Come with me,' Eden commanded.

He rode off at a trot that left Keston and Adrienne hurrying along behind him. The D'Amazone could stand the pace, but Keston soon found himself panting.

They moved through a warren of interconnecting caverns, illuminated by cold-light panels, past underground springs where steam spurted in geysers. It was hot with radioactive heat from the interior and sounds like thunder rumbled far below.

The ground shook violently and the Beast pranced on its hind legs, almost throwing Eden. He cuffed the side of its head.

'Behave, Juvenis!' He glanced back at Keston. 'It's only a quake — they happen all the time here. Nothing to worry about. They're never serious.'

Keston, uneasy, hoped he was right; he did not fancy the idea of being buried alive. They passed through more caverns to Eden's living quarters; the master of the wandering planet dismounted and turned Juvenis free. Keston noted that the Beast did not wander far; it seemed to have its own quarters at the far end of the same cavern.

He was glad to sit down and take stock of his surroundings. The room, vast as it was, seemed an anti-climax. The furnishings were old; probably they had been the latest thing a long time ago, but now they were out of fashion and showing signs of wear. There was dust in the corners, an air of gloom about this place. Along one wall was a library of recordings. A robot, an ancient model, brought synthetic food and ice-cold fruit juice. The food tasted as drear as anything

Keston had tasted back on Terra . . . living alone had made Eden careless of his house-keeping, he decided.

Kyle Eden sat stiffly upright in a high backed chair, gaze fastened on Keston as he began to talk.

'Remember Frankenstein? The world that developed super-robots? They thought they were onto a good thing. Trouble was, their machines put nearly the whole population out of work?' He smirked. 'I was a hero there, you know. It was thanks to me that the unemployed organized and smashed the machines. I think we could do something with that, don't you?'

Keston felt frustrated, almost desperate. Did Eden live entirely in the past? he wondered, and exchanged a glance with Adrienne. She grimaced back.

Bluntly, he said: 'Wainwright has been assassinated.'

'Wainwright?' Eden queried.

'The Director-General of United Worlds.' Didn't he keep up with anything? 'And with Mogul and Technos about to go empire-building, the situation's serious.'

Eden waved a hand. 'Never mind that

now. Let me tell you about the time I — '

Exasperated, Keston interrupted: 'Red-mont, of Technos, is planning to make use of you! He figures to use you — *your* name, *your* legend — as the figurehead for his invasion of other worlds!'

Eden cocked his head to one side. 'Clever, of course, but we can't waste time on that now. We've more important things to discuss. There's the system where I bought and sold a satellite, can't remember the name for the moment, but — '

Keston breathed hard. It seemed he would never get through to this extraordinary man. 'More important than galactic war? You could do something to stop that, perhaps — *now!* Come out in support of UW.'

Eden shook his head. 'I'm just not interested, Keston. Let them fight it out if they want to. And do, please, stop interrupting me!'

Brutally, Keston said: 'Barnabas had the idea you Edens might be finished. I think he's right. There was a time when you'd have been interested.'

150

'A long time ago. I've been at this game too long now to care much for such things any more. Much too long . . . '

Keston stared at him, puzzled by his tone. He looked at Copper, who only shrugged.

Kyle Eden shifted in his chair, stretching himself, smiling wearily. 'You haven't guessed then?'

'Guessed what?' Keston asked irritably.

'There never was an Eden Clan. Just me. I discovered the secret of longevity.'

12

Trail's end

Hew Keston leaned forward in his chair, staring into Eden's lined and weary face. There was a shocked pause, then —

'Longevity?' he echoed, the hair at the back of his neck bristling. Was Eden joking? Had his mind, shut away in these gloomy caverns, finally given way?

'That's not for publication, of course,' Eden said. 'Not that anyone would believe you.'

Keston tried to imagine himself selling the idea to Barnabas, and shook his head. He felt stunned, and turned to look at Adrienne. Even she seemed startled out of her normal composure ... and it *would* explain why the pictures of the Edens were all the same.

Here, below the surface of Eden's World, the fabulous Beast kneeling in one corner, staring at the crinkled parchment-like skin of the man himself, it did not seem so incredible.

Shaken, his voice small and lost in the echoing vault, Keston asked: 'How?'

'By chance — an accident,' Eden admitted 'When I discovered this planet and decided to make it my home, Juvenis was here. The only one of his kind apparently, or the last. I've never learnt which . . . well, later, I found that the Beast gives off a radiation, something new. Under infrared it shows up plainly enough, a glowing aura. And it is this radiation that gives longevity — just so long as I stay close to him.'

Longevity, man's eternal dream of prolonged life, Keston thought. He'd come after a big story, and got the biggest of all. But Eden was right; no one would believe.

How old was Eden then? Alain, Morg, David, Kyle four generations spanning more than a century of active life. Was he slowing down now? All one man . . .

Eden said lightly: 'There was a price to pay, of course. A price I didn't realize until I married the first time. The radiation that gave me longevity also made me sterile — and, in those days, I wanted an heir, you understand. I was building an empire and wanted it carried on after me. The doctor told me emphatically, that was impossible — '

Keston began to understand the missing medical records. Eden couldn't allow that secret to leak out. He remembered Quinn's words: *The Edens murder their wives immediately following the first-born . . . * ' There never had been any births, and he stared, appalled.

Adrienne guessed too. Her tawny eyes blazed as she spat out: 'Murderer?'

Eden nodded calmly, recognizing her existence for the first time. 'That, too, was necessary. Once I'd decided to be my own heir — and somehow I had to cover up my secret — the Lady Sin had to go. The other two later of course.' He grinned crookedly. 'Kyle never married. It was just too much bother to go to. I've nothing left to live for. I've seen it all, and I'm bored. Bored to death!' He laughed at his own joke.

Keston looked round uneasily. Juvenis seemed to be watching them, horned head pointed directly at him.

Eden said: 'Don't worry — the radiation takes time to act. You'll be out of here before you need worry about your heirs. Now, let's get on with the script, shall we?'

Keston choked. After all this, building up a fictitious legend seemed the height of anti-climax. He took a deep breath.

'Maybe you couldn't care less what's happening off-world, but I want to know. Where's your laser communicator?'

Eden pointed, bored, to a far corner and Keston rose and crossed the cavern. It was hot, the floor shook with another tremor. He switched on the set and waited for Neoism to answer —

'I'd like to speak to Mr. Flowers. He's a UW agent staying at the travellers' hotel.'

Minutes later, the reply came: 'Mr. Flowers stetted to Terra when the news broke of Redmont's invasion of Botan.'

'Invasion!' Keston licked dry lips and switched off. Turning, he said dully: 'It's come — the war's started!'

155

Adrienne's face looked set in the glow from the cold-light panels. Eden sighed wearily, spreading his hands. 'Even ten years ago, I might have taken some interest. But now . . .'

A robot brought him a fresh drink and he sipped while Keston restlessly paced up and down the underground cavern.

This was the end of the Federation, the end of United Worlds, Keston thought — and with UW, the end of Terra. Her economy would simply break down. He smacked a fist into the palm of his other hand, glaring savagely at Eden. 'If you'd stepped in on UW's side before, you could have tipped the balance. I'm sure of it. You could — '

He stopped in mid-stride, freezing as an idea came to him. His expression changed, seemed — to Adrienne, watching him with curiosity — seemed to become dynamic. It was as if Keston became, in an instant, a different man. A man of action.

'But we don't need you at all! Nobody's seen you in the flesh for years. Barnabas can fake an image on stereo

— use a robot for the Beast — and your supporters will follow our lead. It can be done. It must!'

He began pacing again, the blood flowing faster in his veins. He had forgotten he was a mere scripter of legends; enthusiasm gripped him.

He appeared somehow taller, dominating the cavern and Eden and the Beast.

'With Eden backing UW . . . come on, Copper, we're leaving now. I'll give Redmont and Technos something to think about!'

* * *

Flowers had been badly disturbed by Keston's report. With Wainwright dead, the outlook appeared bleak for UW — as bleak as the monochrome abstract painted on the wall of his hotel room on Neoism. He brooded until a knock came at the door.

A uniformed stet messenger stood there. Flowers ripped open the sealed message and read: TECHNOS INVADED BOTAN. He scowled, screwing the message-form into a ball . . . was there any point in waiting now?

Deciding not, he made his way to the stet station and returned to Terra. Now that Redmont had taken this irrevocable step, Keston no longer seemed important; not that he'd ever understood why he had been ordered to watch him anyway.

He left the booth and took the lift to the surface; everywhere, the people of Terra gathered in front of stereo screens, discussing the news. They seemed only slightly worried as yet . . .

Flowers arrived at UW headquarters and went directly to the office of his section head. His boss's face registered surprise — field agents rarely showed up at H.Q. without being ordered to. 'Hello, T.S. I wasn't expecting you — but take a seat.'

Flowers remained standing. 'There was nothing to hang around Neoism for. Keston's got his D'Amazone guard with him — and no assassin can get at him on Eden's World, even if anyone's still trying, which I doubt.' He briefed his chief on Keston's story.

'Stet-switch, and Redmont planning to use Eden . . . h'mm.' The head of Field Agencies doodled absently on a pad. 'I'd better tell Neale about this.'

'Neale's got the big job then?' Flowers spoke casually; he'd never liked the man — he was a smoothie, had gone up too far, too fast, leaving better men behind him.

'That's right, T.S. Neale's in the saddle now — and the first thing he does is call off the police action that Wainwright ordered. Some of us don't altogether agree with that — '

'I don't,' Flowers stated flatly. 'If we threw all our weight in on Botan, we might just stop this situation before it gets completely out of hand.'

The chief looked grim. 'It's too late for that. It's busting at the seams — already the Federation's splitting, taking sides. This war is going to spread faster than we can do anything to stop.'

Flowers rubbed his jaw, looking round the office. Empty desks, no phones ringing; he'd expected action here. And the chief looked old, defeated. 'Did he give any reason for cancelling?'

'Oh, the usual — it would be an infringement of the non-intervention pact.'

'Yet Wainwright decided on it and he had a lot more respect for the pact than Neale ever will.'

The chief raised an eyebrow. 'I didn't hear that, T.S. And you'd better get your thinking straightened out if you want to stay with UW.'

'Assuming there's any UW to stay with . . . '

There was a short silence, then Flowers said: 'So what do we do now? Sit on our butts till we're all out of a job?'

'Just till fresh orders come through.'

'All right . . . who killed Wainwright? Have you got him?'

The chief scowled. 'Not yet. Neale said to leave it to the police — but just between the two of us, I've got a couple of undercover men looking around.'

'*Neale said* — ' Suspicion clouded Flowers' mind. Wainwright was killed and Neale stepped into his shoes — and Neale didn't want UW agents probing. He forced himself to speak casually. 'Guess that's it then. Nothing I can do here. I'll grab a bite to eat and some sleep before I go back to Park.'

'Yeah, you do that T.S. I'll be in touch later.'

Flowers walked heavily out of the office, a thickset man with iron-grey hair and worry in his eyes. But he did not leave the building immediately. He'd been with United Worlds a long time and believed in the organization's importance. He was loyal to its ideals — and he'd liked Wainwright.

He went into the staff canteen and bought a drink, carried it to a table. He sat alone, thinking. He had a nice berth on Park as the local agent, so why stick his neck out? Whose idea had it been to send him running after Keston? And why? Was Eden really likely to intervene, and if so, did it really matter?

He sipped his drink and decided he wasn't going back to Park just yet. Not till he'd sorted a few things out in his mind ... perhaps not ever again, he reminded himself. If the Federation fell, United

Worlds fell with it.

Now that Redmont had made his move, Deterling would not be far behind . . .

At another table, nearby, two Terran agents were talking as they ate a meal. Flowers could not help overhearing, and his ears pricked up.

'I hear Neale's changed since he took over — '

'Yeah, the top-man complex.' The speaker chuckled softly. 'Neale of Terra!'

Flowers didn't feel like chuckling. The blood froze in his veins; perhaps it took an off-worlder to see the obvious, or perhaps . . . he put the alternative out of his head. In any case, his mind was now made up.

He strolled to a call booth and dialled a restricted number; an agent always had contacts in Intelligence, the police, Security. He had to.

He ensured the line was scrambled and identified himself before putting his question. 'Neale will have a quiet address somewhere — can you give it to me?'

His contact hesitated. Flowers pleaded

it was a security check. Minutes later, he made certain that Neale was still in his office and set out for Norma's place, following a hunch.

★　★　★

A pall of choking grey smoke hung above the fields and farms of the agricultural world of Botan. The clash of arms echoed through the shrieks of the dying as the invaders raged across the planet chanting the battle-cry: 'For Technos and Progress!'

There was bitterness in the hearts of the defenders; they felt deserted when United Worlds changed its policy at the vital moment, leaving them to fight alone. A neighbouring world, Astron, feeling itself threatened, sent hasty messages of moral support and began to mobilize — this planet, colonized by believers in astrology was no better equipped for war than Botan itself.

Meantime, the women and children fought — and died — alongside the men. Botan, a vast checkerboard of fields and hydroponic beds, was highly mechanized; but agricultural machinery failed against advanced armament.

The invasion swept on, the smell of death pervaded the air, and the farmers withdrew step by reluctant step, burning their crops and homes, leaving only barren victory to the invaders.

Lacking fighting weapons they had the courage and determination to endure to the end. One small advantage they had; the city-bred men of Technos were out of their normal element in open country. So the fighting developed into guerilla warfare; ambush, withdraw, and ambush again.

Still Technos poured in fresh troops, supported by robot soldiers, to take over the planet, driving the defenders back. Time favoured Redmont, for only a miracle could save Botan now.

13

Man of action

Adrienne sat on the edge of *Firefly's* bunk, watching Keston use the winch to trim the silver sail towering above their tiny capsule. The solar wind yacht was tacking back to Neoism. Absorbed in his manoeuvring, he was temporarily unaware of her presence as he played the sailer to get the utmost speed from it. And he was building speed as if he'd done this all his life.

Keston was a changed man, Adrienne thought as she watched him. When she'd first met him, he had been scared — yet he still went on with his job. She was willing to grant him that much. And he'd quickly got over his embarrassment and adapted to having her around all the time.

But the change in him was more than that and she couldn't quite pin it down. There was a dynamic, masterful air about him now that he'd never had before — almost as though he were of D'Amazone, an obvious impossibility. On the whole, she approved of the change; while, at the same time, it irritated her sense of superiority. It was unheard of for a guard of D'Amazone to feel the slightest respect for any man. She reminded herself she must certainly not reveal her feelings when she returned to her own planet.

Eden's World lay far behind them; even the red glow from the dark wanderer's volcanoes no longer gleamed through the port.

Adrienne's thoughts veered away from Eden, not knowing which she considered worse — his fake legend and all it entailed, or the notion of longevity . . . she still refused to think seriously of the possibility of a life stretching over several generations. She was not even sure that she would report it to the Matriarch . . .

Her gaze held steadily on Keston, watching the sail, adjusting the rigging; he had lost interest in his script-work. His purpose had changed, and he with it. Except for one thing, she thought; he still wanted her as a woman. She could tell that, and wondered at it. Men rarely, after the first rebuff, wanted a woman of D'Amazone. It amused her, stirred her in some primitive way . . . something else she dare not reveal at home. Really, she was getting as secretive as the people of Espion . . .

Eden's final words, before their blast-off in the rocket ferry, echoed in her mind. And his tolerant chuckle of amusement. 'A fake Eden! I like that — it'll add something new to the legend!'

Firefly sped on, tacking to take advantage of the wind of light pressure from Neoism's sun, large in the black vault of space. The hours passed and ahead of them, the art-world loomed, a drab brown ball. She could see a glint of metal, the orbital rocket waiting to take them down to the surface.

When had Keston changed exactly? The moment Eden made his longevity claim? Or when the laser message came informing them of the Autarch's invasion of Botan? Redmont . . . a slow anger burned inside her at the memory of her humiliation. Keston should not have made a deal; she found it hard to forgive him that.

Skillfully he sailed the capsule into orbit about Neoism, matching speed with the ferry rocket. Magnetic clamps operated, and she followed him through into the rocket and strapped down. The pilot fired the retros and they fell through the sky towards the planet of the artists.

The rockets fired again just before landing, pressing her deep into the foam couch. The reality of galactic war suddenly struck her; it spelt the end of the Federation and United worlds . . .

They landed. Keston was on his feet, a man in a hurry. He gripped her arm and began to run. 'C'mon, Copper — we're stetting.'

'Where to?'

'D'Amazone.'

Adrienne broke step, staring at him, startled. She realized he meant it and quickened her pace to catch up with him in the transmitting hall.

She stepped into the booth, leaving the olive-and-orange abstract behind — forever, she hoped — and out into familiar surroundings. Two warriors were discussing fighting techniques and she sensed tension in the air; when they saw Keston, they moved swiftly out of sight down one of the many passages.

He staggered momentarily under increased gravity and spoke abruptly to the receptionist. 'I must see the Matriarch immediately.'

The receptionist stared him down. 'Impossible No man speaks with the Matriarch.'

'I will,' Keston said confidently. 'Tell her it's about the war — I've got a plan to stop it.'

The receptionist's stare turned into a sneer. Adrienne found herself looking away, almost desperately; she looked at the tiled floor, the fountain, the passages leading to quarters where no man's foot had ever trod. This was home, inviolate. And she heard herself say, 'It is best, Gwyneth. This is the right thing to do — inform the Matriarch.'

Gwyneth glared savagely at her.

Adrienne took a deep breath. 'I'll take responsibility.'

Gwyneth — reluctant — spoke into the intercom and waited for a reply. She avoided looking at Keston as she gave the answer. 'The Matriarch will receive you, man.'

'Good,' Keston said breezily. 'And tell her to hurry, will you?'

Adrienne gasped, then grabbed Keston's hand and dragged him to the guest room. They waited. She shivered, wondering what had made her speak up; she did not *know* this was the right course. But there was a mantle of power about this man, a power that commanded her . . .

She felt as nervous as she had the night she waited for her warrior's test.

Then the Matriarch walked slowly into the room, grey hair cut short, her back stiff, dagger at her belt. Her short tunic was plain, and her voice had an edge to it. 'Be seated.'

Adrienne bowed, and sat.

The Matriarch lowered herself stiffly, resting her arms on the table, gazing severely at Keston. Adrienne wondered how long it had been since she last set eyes on a man.

'You say you can stop this war. Well, I'm interested. Start talking.'

Keston remained standing, dominating the room. 'I need your help to achieve anything. You'll know that if Technos and Mogul succeed with their empire building, the Federation's finished. And with it, D'Amazone.'

The Matriarch shook her head fiercely. A scar on her seamed face turned pink. 'We'll fight!'

'Of course you will,' Keston said crisply. 'But you can't win alone. Your way of life is not popular throughout the galaxy, and you'll find more than one planet against you. You *need* United Worlds and the nonintervention pact — a lot of worlds do, for that matter.'

'And your plan is . . . ?'

'Fight now — on Botan — under Eden.'

The Matriarch showed her teeth. She half-rose from the chair, spitting. 'Under Eden? A man? Never!'

171

'Under Eden,' Keston said firmly. 'You will, because it's your only chance. Eden alone can hold the Federation together now. He'll have UW backing — I'll see to that. But D'Amazone is the one planet with ready-trained warriors, fighting women who can hold their own against the hordes of Technos and Mogul . . . and the legend of Eden will unite a majority of worlds behind you.'

The Matriarch was silent.

Keston said: 'Redmont has a machine to control stetting from a distance — think what that means.'

Startled, the Matriarch looked at Adrienne.

'It is true, Mother,' she said quietly. 'Redmont took Keston and myself from a stet booth on Honeymoon — we were set-up for Neoism, and arrived on Technos.' The Matriarch began to look worried, and Adrienne hurried on, feeling herself a traitor. 'I believe Keston is right. We cannot stand. We should fight on Botan . . . under the *name* of Eden.'

She breathed relief as Keston came in smoothly. 'Eden will be a fake — just a stereo image, to get the legend behind you. No one's going to interfere or tell you what to do. You'll be in command of your warriors all the time.'

The Matriarch considered this at length, her grey head nodding. 'It is a good plan. There is a chance of success — and I see none without. Very well, we shall fight on Botan.' She winced. 'Under the name of Eden.'

Keston nodded, taking her agreement casually. 'Good! That's settled then. Get your warriors ready — I'll let you know the right moment to strike.'

He took Adrienne's arm. 'Now, Copper, we have to fix things with Barnabas . . . '

Bowing hurriedly to the Matriarch, Adrienne followed Keston out of the guest room and back to the transmitting centre. 'Terra,' he snapped at the operator as she stepped into the booth with him.

Adrienne came out in a vast vaulted hall — below ground, she guessed. There were many rows of booths and the place was crowded with travellers, all seemingly in a hurry. She adjusted the gun at her belt for a quick draw.

Keston strode through the open portal and stepped onto a moving belt. People flashed by, riding the strip. She stepped gingerly after him, trying to keep her balance as she was whisked along. This was her first visit to Terra, and nowhere had she met the rolling roads before. She fought down a feeling of terror as tunnel walls sped past.

Neon-ads flared at her; noise roared. The people of Terra seemed in a mad rush to go somewhere; they darted onto the strip, jumped off. Everywhere was constant change; shops, people, sounds. She gripped Keston's arm to help maintain her balance, and he smiled at her.

'Not far to go, Copper.'

She observed the feminine curves of the Terran girls, soft and boldly displayed. This was Keston's home world, she remembered; this was how he was used to seeing women. Somehow, she felt at a disadvantage.

They arrived at a platform under a large flashing sign that read: STEREO-SCOPICS INC. and Keston helped her off the moving way. They entered a cage that rushed upwards at express speed, pressing the soles of her sandals hard against the floor, almost buckling her legs.

Adrienne was beginning to appreciate that Terrans were always in a hurry. Keston's changed outlook became more understandable — and she remembered that it was from this planet that all the Federation worlds had been colonized, including D'Amazone. These people were her native stock.

The cage stopped and she stepped out into the corridor of a tower building; through a window, she glimpsed clouds and the tops of concrete canyon walls.

Keston moved briskly towards a man seated outside a closed door. 'Is Barnabas in?'

'Yes sir, Mr. Keston, but he — '

Keston pushed past the man, opened the door and walked inside.

Adrienne followed. She saw a big office with an indigo ceiling, a sprawling desk with a massively built man behind it; he was smoking a cigar in a green holder and dictating at speed to a secretary.

Keston interrupted: 'That can wait, Barnabas. What I've got, can't.'

Barnabas stared at him, surprised. Then he dismissed the secretary with a flourish of his cigar. 'All right, Keston, but it had better be good.'

Adrienne was aware of a wave of subtle perfume as the secretary passed her. A young girl, blonde, with willowy curves and tight-fitting dress. Keston would know her, she thought, and felt furious because she was jealous. For an instant, she felt cheated and regretted her own Spartan regime.

The door closed behind the girl, and Keston said: 'I can stop this war, Barnabas. But I need your help.'

Adrienne realized that Barnabas was staring at her, recognized what she was. He said, jerking a thumb, '*She* won't come on your expense sheet.'

Keston ignored the remark. 'You're going to fake an image of Eden and his Beast on stereo — '

'Easy enough.'

' — and get the clan supporters behind us.'

'I can do that too,' Barnabas said calmly. 'A simple promotion job. Now tell me why I should.'

'Eden — our fake Eden — will lead the warriors of D'Amazone against Technos on Botan. Against Mogul too, if that becomes necessary, to prevent the spread of galactic war, uphold UW and save the Federation.'

Barnabas quivered. He crushed out his cigar and rose from behind the desk. His voice boomed with enthusiasm. 'Eden and the guards of D'Amazone . . . yeah, that's good. That's great! Magnificent stereo!' He hesitated fractionally. 'What about UW?'

'They'll have to follow us once we set the ball rolling. The public will demand it.'

Barnabas looked admiringly at Keston. 'Yeah, you've got it. Now, if it were Wainwright, I'd say bring UW in on this now. But rumour says Neale's called off a police action. This way, we can force him to move. I'm with you.'

Keston said: 'Set it up then, will you?' and moved to the door. 'I've another call to make yet.'

177

Adrienne followed him as he left the office. She thought wryly: All she seemed to do since Keston had taken the bit between his teeth was follow him around. It was a disturbing thought for a guard of D'Amazone.

14

A fish is hooked

Keston grinned at Adrienne as the lift dropped swiftly to the stet station. 'You may have to earn your keep this time — to get the sort of action I want, I'm going to have to enter the lion's cage.'

He crossed the hall to a vacant booth. 'Mogul,' he told the operator.

Adrienne followed him through . . . the reception hall on Mogul was a bleak unfriendly place, full of armed men.

Keston said loudly: 'I'm from Terra, here to see Deterling. Take me to him immediately.'

The guard corporal smiled wolfishly, waving his men to close about them. 'Terra, is it? We've been told to expect you!'

Keston frowned, puzzled. How could Deterling be expecting him? Uneasily, he remembered that Redmont had suggested

Deterling was behind the earliest attempts on his life . . .

The corporal spoke into a communicator: 'The Terran's arrived as expected, with a guard of D'Amazone.'

Keston noted thankfully that these men treated Adrienne with caution; the fighting women of D'Amazone had a formidable reputation. Her presence surrounded him with an aura of security.

'Deterling will grant you audience,' the corporal reported.

Keston walked outside, the guards falling in round him. The cobbled streets and shells of burnt-out feudal buildings made the town look as if war had hit it. 'One of the lords thought he could take command,' the corporal said. 'You'll see his head in a minute.'

They marched up the hill towards the grim black-walled fortress at the top. A pale sun warmed the checkered fields and cast a silver light on the waters of a distant river. Then massive stone walls loomed up, and a great gate with a pole beside it; on the pole, a decaying head perched.

'Lord Gould,' the corporal said, with apparent satisfaction. The heavy gates creaked open, clanged shut behind them. 'I hope you know what you're doing,' Adrienne murmured.

They walked along stone corridors where faded tapestries hung, the only light from a few sun-powered lamps, and came to a closed door. Deterling's personal guards leveled guns at them as the door opened and they walked into a richly furnished apartment.

Keston walked boldly forward to the glittering throne where Deterling sat in black uniform, his fleshy face topped by a bald skull. Lips twisted in surprise. 'Who are you?'

Keston paused, thinking: he was expecting someone from Terra. Who? He said: 'Hew Keston, scripter for Stereo-scopic.'

Deterling said: 'I've heard about you — what do you want here?'

Keston smiled. If he'd learnt one thing from Eden, it was how to play off one side against the other.

'I've got news for you,' he answered. 'I

181

was on Technos, just before Redmont invaded Botan. Now, suppose you dismiss these guards so we can talk privately?'

Suspicion clouded Deterling's face and he shook his head. 'No! If you've anything to tell me, out with it.'

'Redmont named me his ambassador to visit Eden — '

'Eden!' Deterling half-rose from his throne, sank back again. For a moment, fear showed plainly in his eyes, then he masked it with an appearance of calmness.

Keston knew he'd hooked his fish. Deterling believed the legend explicitly, and that made the rest of his plan possible. He breathed easier, and the lie slid smoothly off his tongue.

'Redmont's plan is this — to use Eden as a figurehead for his conquest and so gain popular power. Technos and Eden together make an unbeatable combination. And Eden agreed to support him!'

Deterling looked dazed, sick with apprehension, and Keston played the fish on his line.

'You can't stand alone against the pair

of them, so . . . your best chance is to strike at Technos while Redmont's attention is concentrated on Botan. Hit the capital while his main striking force is off-planet. Destroy the threat of Technos and you can build an empire at leisure.'

Deterling sat motionless, his gaze darting round the room, from Keston to the D'Amazone, to his couch, the wall-drapes, his guards. He called for a drink . . .

His spies had already reported Techmen on Botan — that part was true — Technos must be weakly held now. His eyes glittered . . . he must decide and act swiftly if he were to prevent a link-up with Eden.

'You're right of course,' he said, draining his goblet and tossing it aside. 'An excellent plan. The time to take Technos is now, but — ' He turned hard probing eyes on Keston. 'What are you after? How do I know I can trust you?'

Keston maintained a poker face. Deterling could not possibly imagine what it was he really wanted, must not be allowed to learn until it was too late. He said: 'I owe my D'Amazone a favour. Redmont insulted her and she wants his head. That's why we'll be going to Technos with you!'

Deterling glanced at Adrienne and seemed satisfied with what he saw there. He nodded, and turned to an aide. 'Are the invasion forces ready?'

'Yes, sire.'

'Good! Switch the objective — Freedom can wait. We hit Technos, now!'

★ ★ ★

Flowers watched Norma's apartment from a doorway across the street. This was a select part of the city and the house, an old one, was set discreetly back from the traffic lanes. A light showed at the window, but he decided not to wait; he must act while he knew Neale was still at UW headquarters.

He looked round carefully to make sure he was not observed, loosened his gun in its holster, and crossed the road. Evening shadows obscured him as he moved into the apartment house doorway and used a pick-lock.

The door swung open and he slipped quietly inside, sniffed the air; a woman's perfume. The apartment was furnished tastefully. He moved noiselessly to the door of the bedroom.

Norma stretched out languidly on the double bed, a glass on the low table beside her, watching a wall screen; it showed a stereo family going through their routine life. She was about thirty, blonde, her figure carefully preserved, her face vacuous. Flowers guessed she would know nothing of what was going on.

He darted smoothly across the room, thick carpet deadening his approach; one hand rested across her mouth to prevent an outcry, the other chopped edgeways at her temple, reducing her to unconsciousness. He used a sheet to tie and gag her.

Next he walked through the apartment to ensure she was alone. Then he began a methodical search, stripping everything. No need to hide his tracks; he'd only have this one chance to find the evidence he wanted.

But the place was dismally bare of anything incriminating Neale. It was so obviously no more than a love-nest. And time was passing. He stood in the doorway between the rooms, scratching his head, thinking . . . frustrated. Unless he was completely wrong, he had missed something.

Norma came to and glared at him above her gag. Could she possibly know anything? He shook his head and went over the walls, feeling them with his fingertips — and, suddenly, a wall panel moved under his hand. A dark cavity showed beyond.

Flowers glanced back at Norma, saw that her expression revealed complete surprise. So he was right about her . . . he stepped through the gap and found himself in the adjoining apartment.

He moved warily, checked that it was deserted and the outer door locked, then switched on the light. This was a very different place; a workroom, with a desk, dust in the corners, a waste bin filled to overflowing. Neale didn't allow even a cleaner in this secret place.

Flowers hummed happily as he settled to his search. The desk first, locked. He used his pick-lock again, and took out a handful of papers; hand-written, coded. He thrust them into his pocket to be studied later. In one corner he found a communicator with a blanked-off screen; so Neale dealt with somebody undercover and dare not risk revealing his identity.

He opened a suitcase and found a small needle-gun and poison darts. His pulse quickened. Wainwright had been killed by this type of weapon. With luck, there would be fingerprints and the poison would match that which had seen found in the dead UW Director. This was evidence he could use against Neale.

Flowers smiled. At assassination, Neale was the merest amateur. He brought a clean white rag from his pocket and bent over to pick up the gun . . . froze as he felt a draught at his back.

He whirled round, hand darting for the butt of his own gun, silently cursing his overconfidence.

Neale stood in the doorway between the two apartments holding a laser on him. 'I wouldn't take the chance,' the new Director said, watching him intently. Flowers let his hand, now clammy with sweat, drop empty at his side. He counted slowly in his head, fighting for self-control. He felt savage. The game in his hands and . . .

Neale said softly: 'I think you know too much to be allowed to live.'

15

The big con

Keston wore a poker-face as he stood beside Deterling in the stet station below the fortress. He stared at massed banks of stet booths, each one preset to the co-ordinates of Technos — and watched the armed hordes of Mogul pour through without end.

Invasion by stet . . .

Deterling, surrounded by his personal guards, rubbed his hands and smiled broadly. The first reports indicated that his invasion was going well.

Adrienne, behind Keston, remained alert, hand resting lightly on the butt of her holstered laser gun.

At last, a break came in the troop movements. The advance striking force had gone through unhindered; now the engineers moved up their heavy weapons. Keston glanced at Adrienne and said:

'Time for us to seek out Redmont.'

She nodded, wetting her lips.

The guards looked at Deterling as Keston and his D'Amazone moved forward. He grunted, 'Let them go.'

Keston kept the smile off his face. Deterling wouldn't be so casual if he knew what he was really after . . .

With Adrienne beside him, he stepped through the booth, onto Technos. She had her gun out now, ready to protect her client:, but that was not necessary.

Dead Techmen sprawled on the floor of a vast hall, the floor now polished with blood. The only living persons were the soldiers of Mogul. Technos had been taken by complete surprise.

Gunfire blasted and echoed from the streets outside. Keston moved to the doorway and peered cautiously out. The feudal forces of Mogul had fanned out in all directions, taking the battle into the city center and away from the immediate vicinity of the stet station.

Lasers flamed — and it was the weight of sheer numbers of the invaders who carried the fight, so far.

Adrienne nudged him in the back. 'I suppose you're after something — not just giving me a chance at Redmont — so what are we waiting for?'

Keston said: 'We want the stet-switching machine — and I expect to find that's where we'll find Redmont.'

He picked out his bearings and set off down the street towards a high tower. Skirmishes were still going on; most they by-passed. Only once did Adrienne have to use her own gun.

The dust and smoke of battle hung over the city; they passed barricades littered with corpses, a shamble of ruined buildings. Then they seemed to be out of the fighting zone.

A few Techmen hurried towards the tower, carrying weapons. Keston stopped one who seemed to hold superior rank.

'I'm Redmont's personal ambassador to Eden's World,' he said importantly. 'I have vital news — where can I find him?'

The Tech officer, harassed, waved an arm at the tower. 'Research — in the basement.'

Keston and Adrienne walked boldly into the tower building and took the automatic lift down. No one stopped them until they came to a closed door; here, there were guards.

Keston snapped: 'Eden's ambassador. Tell Redmont I'm here.'

The message was passed — and the door opened for them.

Inside, Keston saw Redmont and Quinn and high ranking Techmen gathered about a machine. He touched Adrienne's arm lightly, and murmured: 'Not yet. I've got to find out how this thing works first.'

Redmont was saying, his back to them: 'Hurry, man. Send these invaders back where they come from.'

'Yes, your Reverence!'

Then the Autarch turned, his thin face agitated. 'Ah, Keston, how did you get on? Ignore this trouble — we'll soon put a stop to it.'

Keston went forward, gesturing at the machine. 'This is how you brought us here before?'

'Yes, indeed. And we're preparing to

send these infernal Mogulmen back with it.'

'You can direct them to another world then? It doesn't only bring travellers here?'

'That is so. Control from a distance is simply a matter of setting up space-time-energy co-ordinates. We can redirect them anywhere we choose.'

Keston studied the machine closely; it took the form of a control console, compact and of rugged build. There was a power input and main switch, and dials indicating the three co-ordinates, it looked simple enough to operate, he thought . . .

Redmont said: 'Eden . . . has he agreed to my proposal? Once Deterling has been taken care of, I'll be ready — '

Keston glanced quickly round the underground research laboratory. All the guards were outside; and he had the advantage of surprise.

'So am I,' he said, and nodded to Adrienne

Her laser gun appeared in her hand, covering Redmont. 'Lay hands on a

D'Amazone, would you?'

The Autarch's eyes widened. Quinn lurched forward, and Adrienne burned him.

One of the Techmen darted for the switch operating the stet-switch; Keston grabbed him and hurled him back against the wall.

Redmont said calmly: 'This is foolishness, Keston. You cannot escape from here.'

Keston disconnected the power point of the stet-switch, relieved to find the machine mounted on wheels. 'That's what you think — we're leaving, and taking this machine with us. Try and stop us and — '

Redmont hissed: 'Stop them!'

The Techmen started to move forward and Adrienne's laser flashed again, searing one of Redmont's legs; he toppled, screaming.

The door crashed open and more Techmen poured in. Adrienne beamed them down as Keston put his shoulder behind the stet switch and set the machine rolling towards the open door.

Someone shouted: 'They've killed his Reverence!' In the confusion, Adrienne cleared a path for Keston, as more fanatical Techmen appeared . . .

Keston bawled: 'Men of Mogul! To me, in Deterling's name!'

From the corridor, feudal fighting men came, weapons surging, ferociously attacking the men of Technos. The fight was short and ruthless and left Keston in command.

He addressed the leader of the Mogulmen, pointing at the machine. 'I've got to take this back to Deterling at once — it's a new weapon developed on Technos. I'll need men to help me shift it, and a guard.'

For a moment, the Mogulman stared suspiciously. Then Keston swore at him. 'If Deterling hears of any delay in carrying out his orders, your head will fall! I was sent here especially to get this.'

The Mogul corporal, none too bright, rounded up some musclemen and an escort. Keston, with Adrienne, sauntered behind as his impressed gang pushed the machine along the city streets to the stet station.

Inside, he reset the dials of one of the booths as the machine was carefully manoeuvred in. One of the guards frowned. 'What are you doing?'

Keston nodded to Adrienne. 'Take care of this bunch, Copper.'

Her laser whipped out, covering them. 'Back! We'll take it from here.'

Then Keston and Adrienne, with the stet-switching machine, crossed the space-time continuum, to D'Amazone.

* * *

Flowers stared into Neale's eyes and saw only death reflected there. He straightened up slowly. Play for time was the thought in his head . . .

'I suppose you have an explanation of all this, Mr. Neale?' he asked casually.

Neale laughed. 'I could invent one . . . but between the two of us, why should I bother? I have to kill you, you see that, don't you?'

Flowers gaze went past the new

Director-General, to the secret doorway leading through to Norma's apartment. Empty. That figured. Neale was alone, so he still had a chance.

He brought his gaze back to the young-looking face under grey hair. 'It was you who set killers on Keston's trail, a decoy to set us worrying about Eden and keep our suspicions off your bid to grab power.'

He glanced at the gun in Neale's hand; it was unsteady, and he thought: I can take him — he's strictly an amateur at this game. He tensed to spring . . .

'Norma knows I'm here, Neale. And you can't keep a woman's tongue quiet for ever.'

Neale said: 'I'll take care of her, too.'

Flowers braced himself. There was disgust in him — this was what United Worlds had sunk to . . .

He feinted to the left and moved, fast and violently, to the right. Neale's gun spat a pencil beam, scorching his arm. Flowers mentally suppressed the stab of pain and went in under the muzzle, head lowered. With his full weight and gathering momentum, he rammed Neale in the stomach.

Neale floundered backwards, the air rushing from his lungs in a moaning gasp. His gun fired again, burning a hole in the ceiling. Flowers grabbed for the gun and wrenched it from his hand, reversed it and lashed down with the barrel, hard. Neale sank to the floor and lay still.

Flowers stood over him, sucking in air, feeling the pain burn along his arm. He swayed slightly, and remembered this was the man who had murdered Wainwright. His thumb sought the firing stud as if it had a life of its own; he barely stopped himself from firing at the last moment.

But United Worlds needed Neale in the dock. He, personally, had to be proven guilty before a hundred worlds. Only then could they move to counteract his treachery.

Hell, he had the man, and the evidence. Awkwardly, because his arm hurt, he tied Neale up. Then he walked back through the door to Norma's apartment.

She watched him from the bed, fearful,

and he said briefly: 'If you're not in on Neale's plan, you've nothing to worry about.'

He switched on the communicator to the emergency wavelength and spoke to the police. He gave Norma's address, and his identification number. 'I've got Wainwright's killer here . . . and bring a doctor with you.'

Then, smiling wearily, he sat down to wait.

16

Final plan

The Matriarch of D'Amazone looked thoughtfully from the stet-switching machine, which her technicians were busy studying, to Keston.

'I've no doubt this mechanism will perform as you say it will, Mr. Keston — but exactly how do you propose to use it to our benefit?'

Keston said patiently, as though the answer were obvious. 'Your warriors will transfer to Botan now, and drive the Techmen back to the stetting booths. You can guarantee they'll succeed?'

'Of course!' The Matriarch's eyes flashed in her seamed face and she drew herself up proudly. 'We are trained for war — the men of Technos are the merest amateurs.'

'Very well then. The Techmen withdraw to the stetting booths — in a hurry, I

200

anticipate, now that we've got Deterling to invade their own world. I figure they won't want much convincing it's time to go home.' Keston gestured to the machine he and Adrienne had brought back with them. 'But they won't get home. I'll switch 'em!'

'To where?'

Keston grinned. 'Isn't that obvious too . . . ?'

The Matriarch nodded slowly, and Keston thought: This is Eden's way, setting one against another to scoop the pool. He looked round the hall, at the files of girl warriors waiting patiently the word of command. They looked formidable indeed and he began to feel a little sorry for the invaders on Botan. But they'd brought this on themselves . . .

The Matriarch signalled her commandant. 'Now!'

Eagerly, the D'Amazones moved forward into the pre-set stet booths and the leaders disappeared from view. File after file of tough, well-armed fighting women went to war.

Keston relaxed. So far everything was

201

going as he had planned. He turned to the technicians plugging in the stet-switch to a power point. 'Have you got it figured out yet?'

He received a curt nod.

He watched the files of warriors a while longer, marching from the passages, across the tiled floor, past the fountain, into the booths. Sight of the fountain reminded him he needed a drink.

He turned to Adrienne, and said: 'Let's celebrate . . . if you've got anything stronger than water, that is. *Old Rye*, for preference . . . '

Adrienne glanced at the Matriarch, who looked disapproving. 'We keep a stock of alcohol for guests.'

'That's me,' Keston said cheerfully. 'I've finished masterminding — from now on, events take their course.'

★ ★ ★

Redmont's field commander on Botan was feeling satisfied with the progress of his army as he studied his maps. Three-fifths of the agricultural world was

202

in his hands; though, ruefully, he admitted it a burned and barren land to possess. Still, the guerillas were contained.

He rubbed a hand over his jaw, thinking. Could he now send troops back to settle Deterling's hash at home?

It was a knotty problem, for the farmers fought with desperation, willing to die if they took Techmen with them; and he could not afford to give them encouragement by weakening his forces. A few more days should see the business settled . . .

As he pinned another flag to the wall map in his headquarters, a voice snapped behind him: '*D'Amazones?*'

He wheeled round. His aide, at the field communicator, looked up, worried. 'A report from Gamma sector, sir — they say they're being attacked by D'Amazones!'

The field commander looked blank. 'That's impossible. Who's reporting? Put him on a charge for drinking on duty.'

The aide lifted a hand for silence, listened a moment. 'Gamma sector falling back. The D'Amazones are annihilating them . . . the women are chanting a new battle-cry: For D'Amazone, and Eden!'

'Eden!' Redmont's commander's eyes glazed. 'What nonsense is this?'

But now the communicator *bleeped* continuously. Reports followed one after another . . .

'Alpha sector. More D'Amazones streaming from the stet booths, destroying our robot soldiers!'

'Theta says, Botan guerillas have now joined the D'Amazones. They ask for immediate support!'

The commander took a grip on himself and sounded the emergency siren. As his aides assembled, he snapped out orders: 'Reinforce Theta sector — send the tanks in!'

But the communicator gave him no rest. With each passing hour, fresh and alarming reports came through:

'Beta sector cut off!'

'No more messages from Gamma, sir. Looks as though they've had it!'

The atmosphere in field headquarters

grew tense as reports came in from all over Botan. The D'Amazones were driving the Techmen back, and back . . .

It was nightmare. The commander stared at the wall map, at the shrinking pattern of flags . . .

'D'Amazones heading this way, sir!'

He grabbed his binoculars and strode to the door, flung it open, focused . . . across the fields charged a squadron of mounted girl warriors. He saw his own men, overwhelmed, fall and flee in disarray. Following the D'Amazones came the farmers of Botan, ruthlessly cutting down any survivors.

Lasers flared and brawny muscles wielded cold steel. A plumed D'Amazone in stretch-armour, carried Eden's flag . . .

Redmont's commander rallied his men for a stand, but the fighting intensified. His H.Q. a shambles, he gave ground bitterly, step by step. Still the D'Amazones came on. Now there lay only one avenue of escape. Reluctantly, he gave the order to evacuate Botan.

The beaten Techmen retreated towards the stet booths . . .

Flowers sat in his section chief's office in the UW building on Terra, his arm in a sling. His boss had finally stopped saying complimentary things as news of D'Amazone's interference on Botan broke. Now they both watched the wall screen.

The first pictures, rushed from the agricultural planet, showed fierce fighting between Techmen and D'Amazones, taken from the air. As the camera swooped low above a checkerboard of fields and blasted hydroponic beds, it was obvious that the girl warriors were getting the best of the encounter.

And a good thing too, Flowers thought.

He watched the Techmen break and flee, pursued by D'Amazones . . . and, leading them, rode Eden on his Beast. The handsome Eden of legend.

Flowers gripped an arm of his chair, wondering. Was this really Kyle, come out of his hermitage at long last? Or something Barnabas had faked and superimposed? He remembered the tie-in between Keston and Barnabas. If it was a fake, then it was well done . . . and that meant the ordinary viewer would take Eden's intervention at face value.

He saw the Techmen fall back towards the stetting booths, herded like sheep by the fighting women of D'Amazone. And that puzzled him. It seemed as though Redmont's invading army was being allowed to escape when they could so easily be cut off. He watched them pour through the stet booths . . .

The section chief switched off, smiling. 'We can act now. For once, the Eden legend is useful to us. Intelligence informs me that the majority of Federation worlds are behind Eden . . . '

'If it *is* Eden,' Flowers murmured.

The chief seemed not to hear him.

'Now the new D-G can start a police action against both Technos and Mogul — and make it stick'

* * *

Deterling sat on an improvised throne in his stet station, before massed banks of booths, absently eating fruit handed him by a servant. His mood was a happy one; reports from Technos indicated that his invasion was going to plan. He was mystified by Keston's disappearance, but not seriously alarmed.

He would do well to subdue Redmont before Eden took a hand . . .

Suddenly, he straightened in his chair, frowning as armed men began to come out of the booths. He barked: 'Why are you withdrawing — ?'

And then realized that these men did not wear the feudal black of Mogul. They were Techmen!

The Techmen halted in confusion. They had evacuated Botan, hard-pressed by D'Amazones, and expected to find themselves safely on their own world. There was a moment of bewilderment on both sides, then Deterling howled: 'Kill them! Kill all the Tech dogs!'

His personal guard leapt forward, lasers burning. The Techmen once more grimly fought for their lives — more and more of them came through the stet booths,

208

outnumbering the Mogulmen and pushing them back.

Deterling, alarmed, shouted for reinforcements. Townsmen, hastily armed, came at a run — but still the Techmen kept coming. The battle began to spread, outside the stet station to the town.

Mogul's ruler decided it was time to preserve his skin. Crying, 'Fight to the last man,' he fled up the hill to the safety of his fortress. The iron gates clanged behind him.

What had gone wrong? How had these Techmen got here when his own troops were in control of the booths on Technos? He did not understand it.

He poured himself a drink and gulped it down, climbed the stone steps to a tower. From the rampart, Deterling looked back down the hill.

Desperate fighting was going on. But his men were splitting up, each to support a local lord . . . and Techmen were swarming up the hill towards him.

Deterling began to shiver.

★　★　★

A week after the excitement had died down, Keston and Adrienne sat in the office of Stereoscopics Inc.

Barnabas looked bored as he waved a fat cigar. 'It was good while it lasted, Keston, I'll give you that — but it was all over too soon.'

He began to pace the room. 'Botan cleared by your D'Amazones, Neale facing a murder rap. UW police on both Technos and Mogul.' He seemed to be talking to himself, which was all right with Keston, who sat smiling at Adrienne. 'A new Federation set-up — and one which won't be broken this time — not with UW holding the stet-switch. Anyone get out of hand and — *blooey!* — they're cut off from the rest of the galaxy.'

He stopped pacing a moment to toss out, casually: 'That Eden biography — I've decided to scrub it. Someone might get to wondering what really happened on Botan.'

Keston nodded absently, thinking of Kyle Eden, alone on his sunless wanderer, swinging through the dark void . . . he was welcome to his longevity.

'I've got another job lined up for you,' Barnabas said. 'I'd like you to — '

Keston rose from his seat, still holding Adrienne's hand. She came willingly. He said, shaking his head: 'It'll have to wait — I've a project of my own in mind.'

'Can't it wait?'

'Not this,' Keston said, making for the door with Adrienne in tow. 'I'll see you later.'

Barnabas stared after them as they went out.

Keston dropped to the rolling strip and rode it to the nearest stet station. Adrienne asked with seeming casualness: 'Where to now?'

Keston looked at her. 'I guess I don't need a guard any longer,' he said, 'not now Neale and Deterling are all washed up. So your contract is cancelled.'

'So?'

'So I've got this project in mind. Simple, really. I want to find out if a D'Amazone's aversion of men can be overcome. Specifically, whether you personally can override your upbringing. You follow me?'

211

'I follow you,' she said. 'I think it might be possible . . .'

They arrived at the stet station and joined the queue of travellers. Reaching the desk, Keston showed his seal and said: 'Honeymoon.'

To Adrienne, he murmured. 'After all, it was *your* idea to go back again, Copper.'

She held his hand tightly as they stepped into the booth together.

THE END

We do hope that you have enjoyed reading this large print book.

Did you know that all of our titles are available for purchase?

We publish a wide range of high quality large print books including:
Romances, Mysteries, Classics
General Fiction
Non Fiction and Westerns

Special interest titles available in large print are:
The Little Oxford Dictionary
Music Book, Song Book
Hymn Book, Service Book

Also available from us courtesy of Oxford University Press:
Young Readers' Dictionary
(large print edition)
Young Readers' Thesaurus
(large print edition)

For further information or a free brochure, please contact us at:
Ulverscroft Large Print Books Ltd.,
The Green, Bradgate Road, Anstey,
Leicester, LE7 7FU, England.
Tel: (00 44) **0116 236 4325**
Fax: (00 44) **0116 234 0205**

DARK LEGION

John Glasby

Near the village of Tormount, on Cranston's Hill, Malcolm Amberley had been found dead. He was discovered in the centre of the Standing Stones, clutching the curiously ornamented hilt of a strange dagger, driven into his heart. A curtain of evil hung over the village, a nightmare for Terence Amberley who arrived to attend his brother's funeral. Did Malcolm commit suicide, or did some evil force still remain viable in the area, forcing him towards a mysterious death?

FEDERAL AGENT

Gordon Landsborough

When Inspector Charlie Chey leads the F.B.I. operation to capture the notorious gunman Red Heydendahl, Charlie is gravely wounded and Red is shot dead in the ensuing battle. Criminals, watching the fighting, mistake Charlie for Heydendahl and rescue him, then take him into hiding for medical attention. But how long will it be before the criminals realise their mistake and discover that they've saved the wrong man? And for Red, their vengeance will be swift and terrible . . .

PATTERN OF MURDER

John Russell Fearn

For cinema projectionist Sid Elbridge, it seems that things can't get any worse. First, circumstantial evidence has made him a police suspect in their investigation into a robbery at the cinema where he works. Next, his fiancée Vera is horribly killed in the same cinema, the victim of a falling light fixture. When Sid accidentally finds strange, intricate patterns traced in the dust on the wooden frame of a still case, his curious discovery will reveal a ruthless murderer . . .

SANDS OF DESTINY

E. C. Tubb

In Africa the Foreign Legion stands between the tribesmen with their dreams of the Great Jehad, and the traders and colonists of the peaceful settlements. Secret agent Lieutenant Crispin de Corville discovers a treacherous plot to unite the tribes and wrest arms from the Legion. Fighting his way across the desert, Corville, while in disguise, must learn the tribesmen's plans as he conveys two women to safety . . . realising that the sands of the desert are indeed the 'Sands of Destiny'.